208

465

W9-AVC-738

THE
JENNER
GUNS

THE JENNER GUNS

—A Shawn Starbuck Western—

RAY HOGAN

THORNDIKE
CHIVERS

This Large Print edition is published by Thorndike Press®, Waterville, Maine USA and by BBC Audiobooks, Ltd, Bath, England.

Published in 2005 in the U.S. by arrangement with Golden West Literary Agency.

Published in 2005 in the U.K. by arrangement with Golden West Literary Agency.

U.S. Hardcover 0-7862-7594-4 (Western)
U.K. Hardcover 1-4056-3390-5 (Chivers Large Print)
U.K. Softcover 1-4056-3391-3 (Camden Large Print)

The text of this Large Print edition is unabridged.
Other aspects of the book may vary from the original edition.

Set in 16 pt. Plantin.

Printed in the United States on permanent paper.

British Library Cataloguing-in-Publication Data available

Library of Congress Cataloging-in-Publication Data

Hogan, Ray, 1908–
    The Jenner guns : a Shawn Starbuck western / by
    Ray Hogan.
      p. cm. — (Thorndike Press large print Western)
    ISBN 0-7862-7594-4 (lg. print : hc : alk. paper)
    1. Starbuck, Shawn (Fictitious character) — Fiction.
2. Sheriffs — Fiction.   3. Outlaws — Fiction.   4. Arizona
— Fiction.   5. Large type books.   I. Title.   II. Thorndike
Press large print Western series.
PS3558.O3473J46 2005
  813′.54—dc22   2005002914

THE JENNER GUNS

1

Starbuck, self-conscious in the somewhat outlandish clothing he had purchased in Santa Fe for the occasion, stood in the doorway of the Junction City jail and glanced over the crowd gathered in the street.

He had ridden in shortly before noon, stabled his sorrel gelding, and reported to Homer Beasley and John Duckworth, the townsmen who had persuaded him to accept the job as sheriff and thereby undertake the task of putting an end to the lawless activities of the Jenner gang.

Now, as he took his ease there in the strong October sunlight awaiting the moment to be sworn into office, Shawn Starbuck smiled faintly as the whispered comments and sly observations of onlookers reached him. There was little doubt their remarks were warranted. Clad in a black leather vest resplendent with silver stitching, black corded breeches, the legs of which were tucked inside well-polished boots, also black, a dark blue shirt with a similar-colored bandanna, all topped off with a flat-crowned, wide-brimmed black hat, he was about as far removed from the usual range dress as he could get.

Showy as a peacock, old Hiram Starbuck, his stolid, down-to-earth father would have put it had he been alive to see, but that was the way Shawn had planned it, the reaction he'd hoped for; by sunrise there would be hardly anyone in that part of the territory who did not know Junction City had a new lawman and could not give a full description of him as well.

"He sure is a humdinger, ain't he?"

Starbuck moved slightly, considered the man who had spoken in a tone pitched to be heard throughout the crowd. He was a lean, whiplike man with small, hard eyes, and from the soft drawl in his voice, a Texan. The puncher with him was younger, wore a smirking grin, and sported two guns. Both were garbed as working cowhands.

"You reckon he's as fancy with that iron he's toting as he is with his duds?"

The Texan shrugged. "Sure can't say, but he's carrying it left-handed and tied down. Only the real mean ones do that, I hear tell."

The younger man nodded, jabbed the

bystander next to him with an elbow. "I'm betting nobody ever better cross him! You hear tell what his name is?"

"Starbuck. . . . Shawn Starbuck," the startled man said, drawing back.

"Whooee! With a handle like that he's just got to be the orneriest badge toter there ever was!"

Starbuck smiled thinly. A couple of wise ones, he thought, studying them quietly. A young man yet in years but with the mark of endless disappointments accrued during the so far fruitless quest he was conducting for his brother lying upon his square-cut features, he would like nothing better than to take the pair and knock their heads together until their teeth rattled.

And he would have no difficulty in doing it. Six foot of tempered muscle and bone, expert in the use of his fists as well as the weapon hanging at his side, he had long since learned to hold his own, and more, during the endless treks he'd made back and forth across the raw frontier. A farm boy, born and reared, he had the solidness that came from interminable hours of hard work; he had been adrift and on his own years before reaching majority, and his gray-blue eyes reflected the sureness and confidence that only experience, both good and bad, could instill.

"What do you reckon that fancy belt buckle he's wearing is for?"

It was a different voice, someone in the crowd. The drawling Texan scratched at his jaw.

"Champion something or other, I reckon," he said.

"Like as not got it for dancing with some saloon gal," his partner added loudly with a laugh.

Starbuck's expression did not change. The buckle had belonged to his father, once a skilled practitioner in the art of boxing, a science he had passed on to both his sons. An oblong of scrolled silver on which was superimposed the carved ivory likeness of a boxer in fighting stance, it had been given to Hiram by friends in appreciation of the many weekend exhibitions provided by him. Upon his death, it had been handed down to Shawn.

Stirring, he looked restlessly toward Beasley's General Store, wishing the merchant would put in his appearance and get the ceremony over with. It was in his plan to hold it in the open for all to see, but so great a delay had not been part of the program, and he was nearing the end of his patience, not certain how much longer he could stand idly by and take the jibes that the Texan and his friend were voicing without doing something about it.

He sighed softly. Beasley, in company with John Duckworth, had appeared on the landing fronting the store, were stepping down into the street and coming toward him. Beasley, a graying, sharp-featured man in his mid-fifties, served as mayor of Junction City, while Duckworth, a few years younger and owner of the hotel, was one of its councilmen.

The crowd gave way before them, allowed them to reach the jail and step up onto its narrow porch, take their places beside Starbuck. Duckworth was smiling, but Homer Beasley's face was set and angry.

"You ready?" he asked gruffly.

"Have been for the past hour," Shawn replied, equally blunt. "Where's the deputy?"

"What was holding us up — waiting for Egan," the storekeeper said. "Pretty much put out because we're giving you the job instead of him. . . . Guess he's not coming."

"Forget him," Shawn said indifferently. "Let's get on with it."

Beasley mopped away the sweat accumulated on his forehead. "Ain't so sure this is

11

smart, making all this fuss. That Jenner bunch's going to know exactly what you look like and just how you figure —"

"Was to be no questions asked if I took the job," Starbuck reminded the man in a low voice.

The merchant shrugged, reached into his coat pocket, and produced the nickled star that signified the office. "Only thinking about you and maybe how much more trouble it'll make for you."

"Expect the man knows what he's doing, Homer," Duckworth said wearily. "Let's don't be getting in his way."

Beasley nodded, glanced out over the crowd, and then faced Shawn. "Raise your right hand and repeat after me what I'm saying."

Starbuck complied, echoing, "I swear to uphold the law of the county and the Territory of New Mexico, so help me God."

The storekeeper bobbed again and, reaching forward, pinned the star on Shawn's shirt pocket, avoiding any attempt to affix it to the black leather vest.

"You're hereby appointed to be the legal sheriff of this county, filling out the term of Cyrus Able, deceased, until the next election," the merchant intoned in grandiose style, and stepped back.

A scatter of cheers went up from the gathering. A few voices yelled, "Speech! Speech!"

Shawn raised his hands for silence. "Not much for talking," he said. "Expect to put in my time jailing the outlaws running loose around here."

More cheers sounded. Beasley frowned worriedly. Duckworth smiled, nodded to the crowd as if accepting their plaudits for himself.

"That mean the Jenner gang, too, Sheriff?"

"It does," Starbuck said crisply, replying to the unseen speaker somewhere in the depths of the assembly. "No exceptions."

The drawling Texan, standing a bit apart from the others, hooked his thumbs in his gun belt and spat into the dust.

"You right sure you want to start something with them?" he asked lazily.

"They ain't going to be scared much by fancy duds and hard looks," his partner added warningly.

"Rufe's sure right there," the Texan continued. "It'll take more'n gabbing —"

Starbuck's hand swept down, came up fast. His forty-five rapped loudly in the warm hush. The Texan rocked back as his hat flew from his head, rolled unevenly on its brim into the street.

"Hey!" he shouted, reaching for his own weapon. He hesitated.

Shawn, a half smile on his lips, pistol still leveled, nodded coldly.

"Like I said, don't aim to spend much time talking, only doing."

The Texan let his arm fall slowly to his side. He stared at Starbuck for a long breath and then, wheeling, picked up his hat, pulled it on. Without glancing about, and followed by his friend Rufe, he headed for the horses drawn up at the hitchrack in front of the Ace High Saloon.

The crowd was mostly silent, only a few murmurs of approval being heard. Beasley, features stern, watched Shawn punch the empty cartridge from the cylinder of his gun, reload, and holster the weapon.

"Grandstanding," he said in a low disapproving voice. "It ain't hardly fitting for a lawman to pull a stunt like that."

Starbuck, his eyes on the two riders now swinging off down the street, only shrugged. "Reminding you again of our deal —"

"Not forgetting it," Beasley said quickly. "Only seems to me you're going out of your way to rub folks wrong. Not exactly the smartest idea for a lawman."

Again Starbuck's shoulders stirred. "You happen to know who that pair was?"

Beasley shook his head. "Couple of drifters, I reckon. Don't recollect ever seeing them around here before. Do you, John?"

Duckworth said, "Nope, can't say as I have, but I'm betting they remember us. Specially that long tall one!"

Homer Beasley sighed. "Made us an enemy there. That Texan ain't likely to ever forget."

Shawn remained silent. The smart-mouthed punchers had been more than he'd hoped for and now, inadvertently, had become a part of his scheme. It was said that nothing in that part of the territory escaped the knowledge of Sid Jenner, that he knew of everything that occurred. Accordingly, the fact that Junction City had a new sheriff should reach him doubly fast now, and along with that information, a complete description of the man wearing the star and an accounting of his words and actions at the swearing-in ceremony.

But the game of thoroughly establishing himself, however disagreeable to his nature, in the minds of everyone possible was not over yet. Smiling, he glanced out over the crowd, now breaking up and moving off down the street, and then brought his attention around to Beasley and John Duckworth.

"That deputy of mine never did show up," he said in a loud voice. "You figure he's going to be of any help to me?"

Beasley looked down, stirred uncomfortably. "Don't be too hard on him, Sheriff. Sort of young, but he's a good man, and folks around here like him. Just put out because —"

"I know," Starbuck cut in. "Expected the job himself. Well, he didn't get it, so best thing he can do if he aims to keep wearing that deputy's star is straighten up. Otherwise I'll get somebody else."

"You're right to fire him," the merchant said stiffly.

"Which is just what I'll do," Starbuck promised, and then smiled again. "Well, I guess all this rigamarole's over with. Drinks are on me, so if you'll step over to the Ace High —"

Beasley glanced at Duckworth, frowned. "Obliged, Sheriff, but I'd best be getting back to my store. Maybe later."

"Same here," Duckworth said. "Business sure ain't much, but I got to take care of what little there is."

Shawn nodded understandingly. Everything was going just as he hoped. He might be Junction City's new lawman, but he would be hard pressed to find anyone he could call a friend; even the two town councilmen who had hired him now looked upon him with suspicion and distaste.

"Up to you," he said indifferently, moving toward the edge of the landing. "Offer stands long as my luck keeps holding."

2

Pinning on a sheriff's star and taking up quarters in a fairly good-sized town was a far thought in Shawn Starbuck's mind that day he quit his job as bodyguard for a politician named Flood and headed south. He was pointing for Mexico, there to resume the search for his brother Ben who now called himself Damon Friend, and had scarcely gotten under way when two men hailed him down.

Homer Beasley and John Duckworth they said their names were, mayor and councilman, respectively, of a place called Junction City. They had a proposition for him, and they were prepared to pay him well if he would accept it.

Starbuck had considered them with frank skepticism and a certain amount of impatience. "Finding out these big-paying jobs aren't what they're cracked up to be," he said. "Just walked out on one."

"Heard all about it — and you," Beasley replied. "Main reason why we went chasing after you."

"Ain't nothing like what you was doing," Duckworth added. "And we can't be offering you no real big money like that politician did, but it'll be better'n average."

"What's the job?"

"Sheriff. We've got the authority to appoint you to take over. Interested?"

Appointment to a job to which a man had to be elected; such could only mean that he'd be hanging a dead man's star on his vest, one who had probably been murdered since the town was willing to pay extra for a replacement.

"Could be," Shawn had said, swinging off his saddle and pointing to the deep shade of a nearby cottonwood. "Let's talk about it."

"We've got us a big problem," Beasley began when they were out of the lowering sunlight. "Junction City's a fine town. Was going good, then it all come to a stop."

"Why?"

"Outlaw named Sid Jenner — him and his gang. Moved into our part of the country about two years ago. Come from somewheres up in Kansas, I hear."

"Just plain took \over," Duckworth said. "Now got everything going just how he wants it."

Shawn rubbed at his jaw. "One bunch of

outlaws able to do that? How many in the gang?"

"Hard to say. Some claim there's only a half a dozen; others put it at twice that many. Fact is they're just hard to keep tabs on. Six or eight of them'll hit a stagecoach one day, then maybe next day a bank in a town fifty miles away'll get cleaned out. Don't know if it's the same gang or not. Always wear masks and long dusters."

"I figure there's just one bunch," Duckworth said. "That Sid Jenner's smart, knows how to run things. Real old hand at the business."

"Sure smarter'n everybody that's tried laying him by the heels, that's for certain," Beasley said morosely.

"You talk to Bill Granett, the U.S. marshal about it?"

"We have — quite a while back. He spent some time with us in town, tried to do something about it, but Jenner just laid low. Marshal finally had to leave saying he had the whole territory to look after and that it'd have to be up to our local lawman."

"And then the day after he rode out the Jenners robbed the general store in Briscoe, town east of us," Duckworth said. "Shot up two men, done a lot of other damage besides taking about two hundred dollars. We figure Sid Jenner done it just showing off for the marshal's benefit."

"What about the army? Thing like this happens, they'll usually take a hand if asked."

"Called on them — Fort Union. They sent us over a detail, and they hung around for a month or more looking for Jenner's hideout."

"Never did find it — nobody ever has," Duckworth finished. "Army finally had to pull out."

"Not faulting them or the marshal, either," Beasley said. "Done what they could, and it sure ain't that they don't want to catch Jenner. Hell, besides all the robberies and holdups, they've killed ten or twelve men, so they're wanted for murder, too. It's just that nobody can ever seem to do anything about Sid Jenner. He's always a jump ahead and somehow knows everything that goes on."

Starbuck considered it all thoughtfully. Then, "My job would be to find this Sid Jenner and put a stop to him and his gang, that it?"

"Just what it'd be," Beasley replied as if relieved to have it all said in plain words. "We've got — or leastwise, we had — big plans for our part of the territory. We're sort of away from the capitol, and nobody there pays much attention to us, far as politics go, but we ain't minding that. Sort of always had to look out for ourselves.

"We got a fine thing going for us. There's quite a few ranches in the area, and there's a lot of Texas cattle growers who find it easier to come across the line and trade in Junction City rather'n going clear to Dalhart or some place like that to do their buying —"

"And we sort of had the promise of the railroad coming through, too," Duckworth said. "Would sure mean everything for us — a lot of new people moving in, more business and money for everybody."

"Had?"

"We've got the feeling they're about to change their mind about it," Beasley said heavily. "Can't say as I blame them, either. Be fools to choose a route that's controlled by a gang of murdering outlaws. Expect they have enough of that kind of trouble without going into it purposely."

"What's more, we stand a chance of losing the stage line," Duckworth said. "Know that to be a fact since I'm in the hotel business. Just getting too risky to come through Junction City."

"We lose the stage route, we all might as well lock up shop and move on," Beasley murmured. "You're our best hope, Starbuck. We was on our way to see Marshall Granett about recommending somebody to fill Cy Able's job — he was our sheriff. Got himself bushwhacked about a month ago."

"Don't you have a deputy? Job as big and important as this sounds —"

"Just it, the job's too big for Troy — Troy Egan. He's the deputy. That Jenner bunch would chew him up and spit him out in little pieces if he ever got lucky enough to run them down."

"But you figure I can do something about them?"

"If anybody can, I reckon it'll be you."

Shawn frowned, stared out over the rolling plains. The heat had now broken, and a coolness was setting in. "You don't know me. How can you say that?"

"Going by what we heard there in Bonnerville — and from what we saw happen in the hotel. Too, were told that Granett sent for you to look after that fellow Flood. That right?"

Starbuck nodded. "Was over in Arizona. . . . This Jenner bunch seem to hang out in any particular part of the country?"

"Town called Hackberry, so we've heard, but nobody's ever been able to say for sure. Ain't much more'n a wide place in the road about a day's ride south of us. Army couldn't find them around there, and Cy Able couldn't, either, but Cy was sure they were doing their holing up somewhere's close by."

"He figured they do their trading there," Duckworth continued, "and that the townfolks know who they are and what they are, but they don't say nothing, just keep their traps closed when the law comes sniffing around. In turn, the Jenner bunch leaves them alone — sort of a you-scratch-my-back, I-scratch-your-back arrangement."

"Nothing much there for them to grab was they ever to take the notion, anyway," Beasley said. "Ain't no general store no more or nothing like that since the mines all petered out around there. Fellow named Dooley runs a saloon. Was a livery stable. Ain't sure it's still there. If the Jenners are somewhere close, they'll be doing their buying in Jonesboro or some other town —"

"Maybe even in Junction City. We wouldn't know one of Jenner's guns if he walked down the middle of the street — or Jenner himself, either, for that matter."

"Well, Hackberry's a place to start, and that's something," Starbuck said.

Beasley leaned forward eagerly. "That mean you'll take the job?"

"Can use the money," Shawn said, "and I've got a couple of ideas —"

"Good! Like I told you, we're willing to pay top wages to get the right man," the merchant said, and turned to Duckworth. "What do you think, John?"

"I think we've found the man we're looking for, so let's not mess around. Start at the top — two hundred a month and found."

Beasley swung to Starbuck. "How's that sound? Two hundred dollars a month, your quarters, and take your meals at the hotel's restaurant."

"Fair enough," Starbuck said.

"You do the job up and you're as good as elected to keep on wearing the sheriff's badge long as you want!"

"Afraid I wouldn't be interested in that — in staying put in one place, I mean."

"Up to you. Job'll be yours if things turn out right and you want it. When can you start working?"

"Like to have a couple of days or so," Shawn said. "First have to ride up and do some talking to Marshal Granett —"

Beasley shook his head. "Won't get no help from him."

"Not expecting any, just need to get a few things squared away with him." Starbuck paused, studied the two men quietly. Then, "Something we'd best get clear right now: I want a free hand in this — and no questions asked."

Duckworth nodded immediately, but Homer Beasley was not so readily agreeable. "Being the town council, we ought to know what you figure to do."

"Whatever it is it'll be for the sake of the job and all aimed at bringing in Jenner and breaking up his gang. Might seem odd to you, maybe even wrong, but don't fret over it. I'll be doing what's necessary."

"Still like to know something about your plans."

"Haven't got them worked out yet — leastwise, not completely," Starbuck said, brushing aside Beasley's request. "Maybe just as well you don't know them, anyway. No chance, then, for a leak."

The merchant bristled. "You saying that I —"

"Only repeating what you've told me — that this Jenner knows about everything that goes on around here. Long as I'm the only one knowing my plans, there'll be no chance of him finding out what I intend to do."

"He's right, Homer," Duckworth had said. "We hired him to call the tune, now let's let him do it his way."

And that was how it had ended. The two merchants had headed back to Junction City, while Starbuck continued on to Santa Fe. There he went into a closed-door conference with Granett, the federal marshal, outlining briefly to the lawman his scheme to bring down the outlaws and enlisting his promise of aid when and if it became necessary.

That done, and assured that Granett would say nothing about it, Shawn then sought out one of the larger stores where he outfitted himself with the clothing he felt would best serve his purpose — the kind that made him easily recognizable and long remembered. The purchase reduced his capital to an alarmingly low point, but he gave it no thought; he would have no expenses in the days ahead, and he would be well paid for his efforts; therefore, he could afford to splurge.

His errands in Santa Fe completed, he returned to Junction City, arriving on time and in accordance with the letter he had forwarded by stagecoach to Beasley. The ceremony had been performed as he had directed in the note, and now, with it all behind him, he stepped off the landing fronting the jail and moved slowly toward the Ace High Saloon. The first stage of the plan had been completed. All he could do was await developments.

Nodding to several men along the street, accepting their somewhat restrained congratulations and best wishes with a broad smile, he reached the saloon and, crossing the wide porch, shouldered his way through the swinging doors.

A dozen or more patrons stood at the counter, while a similar number were seated at the nearby tables. All turned to face Starbuck as he entered. Halting in the center of the smoky room, he swept off his hat with an exaggerated flourish.

"Belly up to the bar, gents, drinks are on me!" he called in a loud voice. "Ain't every day a man gets himself made a badge toter!"

3

There was a shout of approval, and those not already at the long polished counter moved hurriedly to find a place.

"Luck to you, Sheriff!" a man called as he raised his glass.

Shawn took up the rye the bartender had set before him, held it aloft.

"*Salud!*" he said, and downed the strong liquor.

"You taking right out after that Jenner bunch?" someone asked as the saloonkeeper started a round of refills.

"No big hurry," Starbuck replied indifferently, tossing a gold eagle onto the counter. "They've been around for quite a spell, doubt if they'll be moving on soon."

A silence fell over the room, broken only by the quiet shuffling of feet, the muted chink of glass. Shawn could almost feel the hostility suddenly present.

"Thought the reason Homer and the town council brought you here was to track down that gang of outlaws, put them out of business."

Starbuck pulled back from the counter for a better look at the speaker. A middle-aged man in a dusty brown suit. One of the local merchants, no doubt.

"Already said I'd be doing that, and I will — in time. Maybe being in a rush is what bought the sheriff you had before me a pine box in the boneyard."

"Cy was a good man," the merchant said stiffly, placing his half-empty glass on the counter with solid emphasis. "I don't take kindly to anything being said against him. None of us do. Cy tried hard, just ran out of luck, that's all."

"Not talking against him, just saying what might've happened. Man can move too fast sometimes."

"And maybe there's them that don't make no moves at all," someone said pointedly.

"I will, come time," Shawn said lightly, picking up his change. The murder of Cy Able was a touchy subject, he was realizing, and his offhand attitude toward it and the outlaws who had committed it was not setting well with the men in the Ace High. "Where was the sheriff when he caught that bullet?"

"Was a ways this side of Hackberry. Broad daylight. He'd been there doing his job, trying to dig up something on the Jenners. One of them potted him from the hills when he was heading back."

"Man should've known better than to do his riding out in the open when he's doing that kind of work."

Several of the men at the bar wheeled abruptly, started for the door. Starbuck cast a shuttered glance at those who remained. Their features were angry. He didn't blame them, would have felt the same as they, but this was the way he wanted it to be.

"Anybody for another round?" he asked cheerfully.

There were no takers. Three more of the saloon's patrons moved for the exit; the group that had been at tables in the beginning returned to their chairs. Suddenly, Starbuck was alone at the counter. He winked broadly at the bartender busily involved in wiping up the wet circles left by glasses.

"Another rye, friend."

The aproned man reached for a bottle, supplied the necessary drink. "Be four bits, Sheriff," he said.

Starbuck flipped the coin to the man, began to twirl the shot glass of liquor between a thumb and forefinger.

"Can't figure why nobody's ever got a look at any of the Jenner bunch," he said thoughtfully. "Yet folks keep telling me he knows everything that goes on in this part of the country."

"How it is," the bartender said. "Got spies everywhere, seems."

"Little hard to believe," Shawn said bluntly, and then as the man behind the counter looked up angrily, added: "Oh, I'm not doubting you — just seems strange. They ever raid this town?"

"Twice. Robbed Beasley's store one time, Grimshaw's bank the other. Made a plenty good haul both times."

"You see it happen?"

"Nope, wasn't here then. Been told about it."

"The sheriff around?"

"Was up the road a piece. Somebody sent for him about some cattle getting shot up — that was the time the bank was cleaned out. Everybody figured later that it was the Jenner bunch that done it, that it was them that sent for Cy Able and got him out of the way. . . . Don't know how it was when they robbed Beasley's."

"And they got away scot-free both times —"

"Yeh, sure did."

"They take quite a bit of cash from the bank?" Shawn asked, leaning forward intently.

"Better'n ten thousand dollars."

"Ten thousand! They always carry a lot of cash on hand like that?"

"Usually do. Grimshaw's got a couple other banks. Sort of supplies them every now and then." The bartender paused, frowned. "Why you asking all them questions about the bank?"

Starbuck shrugged. "Man needs to know something, he asks."

The saloon man resumed his scrubbing of the counter. "Well, you want to know any more about the banking business, you go ask Grimshaw."

"Sure," Starbuck said easily, and tossed off the liquor.

"Sheriff —"

At the word Shawn set the empty whiskey glass on the bar and turned. A dark, intense-looking man a few years older than himself and wearing a deputy's star was standing before him. He nodded briskly.

"You're Troy Egan, I take it."

The lawman made no reply, simply stood and waited.

"Waited for you at the swearing-in ceremony —"

"Had work to do," Egan cut in bluntly, making no secret of his ill feelings. "Rode in a few minutes ago."

"From where — the yonder side of the livery stable or maybe the hotel?" Starbuck asked sarcastically.

The deputy's mouth tightened. Shawn folded his arms across his chest, fixed the man with a cold stare.

"Best we get things straight, Egan. It makes no difference whether you like me or not — I'm the man they pinned the star on. Must've not figured you big enough to take on the job, or they would've given it to you and not come to me.

"Now, you can either get your head screwed back on straight, or you can quit. Won't make a damned bit of difference to me because, far as I'm concerned, deputies come a dime a dozen. Just that I want to know where we stand before we get any older."

Troy Egan's features had reddened. He glanced at the bartender, then to the silently watching men at the tables. After a moment he brushed nervously at the sweat collected on his forehead.

"Aim to keep my job —"

"You will if I say so, and that depends on how good you do your job. That clear?"

"Clear," Egan murmured. "Mighty sorry I had to miss the swearing-in —"

"Maybe you are, and maybe you're not," Starbuck snapped. "But you'd best start

34

remembering beginning right now that I'm running things, not you, not your old boss who let himself get bushwhacked, not anybody else — only me. Savvy?"

Totally crestfallen, Egan bobbed his head slowly. Shawn, maintaining the pretense of being hard, unreasonable, and thoroughly disagreeable, swung his attention to the bartender.

"The deputy'll have his drink now."

The man behind the counter filled a shot glass, shoved it forward. Egan stepped up to the bar, downed the liquor.

"Obliged," he said in a low voice as Starbuck laid a coin beside the empty glass. "Come here to get you, Sheriff."

Shawn's brows lifted. "That so?"

"It's the mayor — him and John Duckworth. Want to see you."

Starbuck shrugged. "They in a big hurry?"

"Reckon so. Told me to bring you to the hotel right away."

"They say why?"

"No, sure didn't."

"Well, expect that means I got to go to work," Shawn said with a deep sigh. "Was sort of planning on taking it easy rest of the day. . . . Come on, Deputy, let's see what it's all about."

4

Egan led Starbuck to a room at the back of the hotel's lower floor, one that evidently served as an office for John Duckworth. As they entered, the hotel owner, Beasley, and a third man were standing at a window looking out at someone in the alley behind the structure. All turned to face him.

Homer Beasley's features were grim. "Not getting any good reports on you, Sheriff. Seems you've been doing some hard talking."

"Didn't know the job called for me keeping a button on my lip. Habit of mine to say what I think. If somebody's toes get tromped on, tough."

Beasley glanced at Duckworth, gestured helplessly. The hotel man smiled wanly. "Guess it don't really matter, Homer, long as he can do the job."

Starbuck frowned. "That what you called me here for?"

Junction City's mayor shook his head, pointed at the third man. "Want you to meet Charley Grimshaw. He's the town's banker. Owns a couple more down the valley."

Shawn extended his hand, forcing Grimshaw, a slightly built individual with round, unblinking blue eyes, to respond.

"My pleasure," the banker murmured.

"Same here," Starbuck said heartily. "Always like to meet a man that fools with cash money. Keep hoping some of the gold caught in his calluses'll rub off onto mine."

Grimshaw smiled weakly, shifted his attention to Beasley who nodded, turned to Shawn.

"You know where Rockville is?"

"Never heard of it."

"Well, it's a town about a day and a half's ride southeast of here. Grimshaw's got a bank there."

"It in this county?"

The merchant nodded.

"Then I reckon it's one of my towns. There something you want done?"

"There is," Beasley said. "Grimshaw's sending a shipment of money to his place there. Want you to take it."

Starbuck frowned, rubbed at his jaw. "Little out of the ordinary to have a county sheriff being a messenger for a bank, isn't it? Seems the bank ought to have its own man or else do the shipping by stagecoach."

"What I used to do, use the stage," Grimshaw said. "Lost the last three shipments. Just can't afford to chance it anymore, leastwise as long as the Jenner gang's running loose."

"Could hire your own rider — two or three if you figure there's need."

"Know that, but finding the right man's the big problem — and when you do, they back off quick soon as they hear about the Jenner bunch. Reason I've appealed to the mayor and the town council — happens I'm a member."

"Makes it handy," Starbuck said dryly, and swung his glance at Beasley. "Expect it's up to you. If you want to use the county sheriff to run errands for your friends —"

"Not the way of it at all!" the merchant protested. "Bank's important to this town, same as it is to Rockville or any other place. Only right to lend a hand when it's needed. Besides —"

"Don't need to hear your reasons," Shawn cut in curtly. Luck was again going his way; this was the second good break to befall him, but it was only wise to appear disgruntled and reluctant. "You want it done, I'll do it. How big's the shipment?"

"Seventy-five hundred dollars, gold and

currency," Grimshaw said. "Don't see that it should matter to you how much."

"Amount doesn't. Was wanting to know how big so I could tell whether it can be carried on a saddle or if I'd be needing a buggy."

Grimshaw drew a handkerchief from his pocket, mopped at his brow. It was close in the small room, and Duckworth turned to open the window. He paused at Beasley's command.

"Leave it shut, John. Could be somebody out there listening."

The hotel man nodded. "Expect you're right. Jenner always gets the word somehow."

"He'll be getting a surprise instead this time," Starbuck said confidently. "What about the shipment?"

"You'll be needing a buggy," the banker said. "It's a fair-sized chest. There'll be some supplies in it — books, papers, and such — along with the money, which will be in a smaller cash box."

"I see. When do you want it done?"

"Tomorrow — leastwise I'm hoping you can do it that soon. Been holding off the shipment since Cy Able was shot, but Rockville's needing that cash and the supplies, and I can't let it go much longer."

Grimshaw paused, looked anxiously at Shawn. "There a chance you can manage it?"

Starbuck shrugged. He would prefer to let all such matters ride for a few more days, but he supposed there was really no need; he had made so great a spectacle of himself since arriving in Junction City that Sid Jenner and his guns undoubtedly were aware by then of his presence.

"Why not? One day's as good as another, far as I'm concerned," he said in an off-hand way.

"Good! Then it's settled," Beasley said, slapping his palms together. "Now, you got any special plans on how you'll do it? Rockville's sort of in Jenner's part of the country."

Starbuck smiled. "Been told he pretty well covers most of the territory around here, but that don't mean anything to me. Aim to get the shipment through, come blizzard or brimstone." Shawn shifted his attention to Troy Egan, waiting near the door in silence. "Be wanting you riding shotgun for me."

The deputy nodded. "Yes, sir."

"And I'm leaving it up to you to get us a buckboard and pick us a good, strong horse. Might have to make a run for it."

40

"What about a posse?" Duckworth wondered. "You figure it'd be a good idea?"

"Be a mistake," Beasley said before Starbuck could make an answer. "Would be sure to draw Jenner's attention. They see only a couple of men going across country in a buckboard, like as not they'll pay it no mind. A posse'd be a dead-sure giveaway. That what you say, Sheriff?"

"That's how I see it," Shawn agreed, relieved. A party of armed riders escorting him and the chest of bank money was the last thing he wanted; such would completely void the scheme he was building to trap the outlaws.

"Who all is going to know about this?"

The men exchanged glances. Grimshaw said, "Just us and Turlock, my bookkeeper."

"He a man you can trust?"

Grimshaw nodded. "Been with me five years or better. Trust him with my money every day of the week. Can see no reason why handling this shipment would be any different."

"Up to you," Shawn said, touching each of the other men in the room with his eyes. "Any chance there'll be a leak on your part?"

Duckworth and Beasley reacted indignantly, the mayor swearing harshly. Egan shook his head.

"Can depend on me not mentioning it, Sheriff."

"How'll you explain renting a rig?"

"Won't have to do no renting. We'll use my pa's. He's down El Paso way doing some visiting."

"It a good outfit that won't be falling apart?"

"Just about new, and's set up for a team."

"That team of Joe Egan's is about a fine a span of horses as you'll come across," Duckworth volunteered.

"Sounds good," Starbuck said, and swung back to Charley Grimshaw. "You fix it so we can load up before daylight?"

"No trouble at all," the banker said. "I'll get Turlock busy at it right away. You can pull up to the back door anytime after dark and start —"

"We'll wait till morning," Shawn cut in. "Don't want the responsibility of all that money on my shoulders any sooner than necessary. Four o'clock all right with you?"

"I'll be there," Grimshaw said, again wiping at the sweat on his lined features.

Starbuck nodded to the remaining men in the room. "Reckon we've settled it. Just asking you be sure to keep quiet about this. . . . Deputy, I'll see you in the morning at the bank — ready to go."

"Sure enough. There anything else you want me to be doing?"

"That team and buckboard's going to be mighty important. It'd be smart to look them over close."

"Just what I'll go do first thing. Anything comes up, where'll you be?"

Starbuck moved toward the door. "Oh, like as not in my office looking things over. If you don't find me there, then try the Ace High. I'll be in one or the other."

Continuing, Shawn smiled faintly at the expressions his words had aroused on the faces of the men in the room. To their way of thinking a saloon was no place for a lawman to idle away his time, and he was inclined to agree, but in this instance it was necessary.

5

They rolled out of Junction City well before daylight that next morning and took the road south for Rockville. The chest containing supplies and cash reserves for Grimshaw's bank was behind the seat of the buckboard, a square of old and stained canvas thrown over it. To the casual observer Starbuck and Troy Egan were simply two ranch hands enroute to some distant point.

In silence, each wrapped in his own thoughts, they moved steadily on through the early-morning chill, but when the sun finally broke over the ragged horizon to the east, flooding the clean sky with a blaze of color and warming the crisp air, the wall between them began to dissolve.

"Brought along some coffee and the making gear," the deputy said. "Figured a swallow or two'd taste mighty good along about now. If you want to pull up —"

"Ought to hit the spot, sure enough," Starbuck said, swinging the team of blacks off the road into a small coulee. "Got a twisted trace that needs straightening, anyway."

Drawing the rig to a halt, he wrapped the lines about the whipstock and dropped to the ground. Egan was down before him and, circling the buckboard, was lifting a small box from under the tarp.

"Brought some meat and bread, too," he announced.

"Coffee'll do fine for now," Shawn said, working at correcting the harness. Egan's rig was a good one, he saw, looking at it now in the daylight. It had been altered and strengthened for more general use and, being heavier than the usual single horse-drawn vehicle, would be much more comfortable on a long journey.

Going over the rest of the leather and finding all in order, he turned to where the deputy was hunched beside a small fire. A blackened coffee pot was nestled in the briskly burning wood, and the water inside it was already beginning to simmer. Egan glanced up as Starbuck moved in beside him, bobbed slightly.

"Be ready in a minute."

"No hurry," Shawn replied, settling down on his heels.

The deputy appeared to have lost his feeling of resentment, now was friendly and cheerful. He was a likable man, and Shawn regretted the hard-nosed brusqueness he had visited upon him that previous day and was not looking forward to what was yet to come. But there was no way around it; once it was all over and done with, he'd make his explanations to Egan — assuming he was alive and able to do so.

"How long've you been a deputy?"

"Only a couple of years," Egan replied, dumping a handful of crushed coffee beans into the pot of boiling water.

"Like being a lawman?"

Troy gave that thought. "Fact is, I do. Hope to keep right on wearing a star. Lawing what you do regular?"

"Nope, done a little of everything."

Egan set the pot off the fire, drew his knife, and flipping back the domed lid, stirred down the surging brown froth. Taking one of the tin cups, he filled it with steaming liquid and passed it to Starbuck.

"You aim to stay with the sheriff job in Junction City?"

It was a quiet, carefully worded question filled with meaning. Troy Egan still felt he should have been the one appointed to fill out the unfinished term of Cy Able, had hopes that it would yet come to pass. Starbuck smiled.

"Not likely. Little hard for me to stay put in any one place."

The relief coming over Troy Egan was noticeable. "Was just wondering," he murmured, filling his own cup with coffee. "Always had a sort of hankering to just drift around myself, see the big towns, meet a lot of folks."

"Not all it's cracked up to be," Shawn said. "Man can get mighty tired of going nowhere."

"Then why do you do it?"

"Happens I'm looking for my brother. Been at it for quite a spell now and was about to get around to asking you about him. Could be you've seen him. Goes by the name of Damon Friend."

Egan sipped at his coffee while a frown knitted his brow. Finally, he shook his head. "Nope, don't recollect nobody with that name. He a stepbrother?"

"No, real name's Starbuck, same as mine. Ben Starbuck. Started calling himself Friend after he left home."

"Family quarrel or something?"

"Yeh, between him and my pa. He was about sixteen then — around twelve years ago."

Egan's frown deepened. "You been looking for him ever since?"

"Just since Pa died. You real sure he was never in your town? He could've used

47

some other name besides Friend, but I understand we look quite a bit alike — he'd be heavier and a little shorter. Like as not he would have put on a boxing match."

The deputy gave that thought, again shook his head. "Nope, I'm sure. Why you so bent on hunting him down? He do something wrong?"

Starbuck smiled at the bluntness of the question but he let it pass. Troy Egan was young at the game; he'd learn.

"My pa's estate — can't settle it until I locate Ben and take him back to sign some papers."

Troy fell silent, eyes on the contents of his cup. After a time he reached for the pot, refilled his tin container, offered more to Starbuck who declined.

"That all you do — ride around the country hunting him?"

"When I'm not working somewhere. Have to pull up when I run out of cash, take a job. Once I've got myself a new stake, I move on."

"And that's what you're doing now, working to get some money ahead —"

Starbuck nodded. "What it amounts to."

Again relief was apparent in Troy Egan's eyes. He clucked softly. "Bet you can say

48

you've sure seen the elephant a plenty of times!"

Shawn drained the last of his drink, tossed the empty cup back into the box Egan had taken it from.

"From the Mississippi to the California sea, Mexico to Canada. Get a tip now and then on Ben and always run them down. Come close a few times but never quite caught up. . . . Expect we'd best get moving."

Egan tossed off the remainder of his coffee, dropped the cup into the carton alongside Starbuck's. Emptying the pot onto the fire, he added it to the box and returned all to the buckboard.

Shawn, climbing onto the seat and gathering up the reins, waited until the deputy was beside him and then cut back to the road.

"How long before we get to where we might run into Jenner?" he asked when the team was again under way.

Troy pointed to a blue haze of mountains well ahead. "Their hangout's somewhere in those hills."

"We go by there?"

"Not quite. Road forks four or five miles inside them. Right-hand goes on to Hackberry, left one takes you to Rockville and on to Texas."

"Then if we're running in luck and get onto that left fork without the Jenner bunch spotting us, we'll make it with no trouble?"

"Maybe. Him and his bunch're all over the place, not just on the Hackberry road. Like as not they're taking a look at us right now."

"I see. . . . He know you?"

"Can't say. I sure don't know what he looks like or any of his bunch, either, for that matter."

"Well, best we play it safe. That star you're wearing, put it in your pocket where it won't be catching the sun and showing up so good. And that rifle, keep it down behind the dashboard. No point advertising that we're moving a valuable cargo."

Egan nodded, complied without comment as they rolled on, the team of blacks moving at a good pace. At noon they halted again for more coffee and a bite of lunch, taking advantage of the break to rest the horses. But within an hour they were once more under way, bearing now directly toward the mountains gradually becoming distinct.

It was midafternoon when they reached the towering formations of rocky peaks and pine-clad slopes, and at once Starbuck became aware of a change in the deputy. He had become tense, was hunched forward on the seat, hands gripping the barrel of the rifle, now propped upright between his knees, so tightly the knuckles shown white through leather-brown skin. He was staring straight ahead.

Shawn studied the man quietly. Although Egan was undoubtedly older than he, the deputy's lack of experience was showing in those moments. He understood now why Homer Beasley and the rest of the town council had looked elsewhere for their lawman.

"Ease off," Starbuck murmured. "No need to get all tight."

"Jenner — he's bound to be around here close," the deputy said. "Just got a feeling he's watching us right now."

"Far as he can tell, we're just a couple of pilgrims headed for town. Acting like you are — all primed to jump up and start shooting at the first jackrabbit that moves — he'll guess right off that we're something else."

Troy sank back into the seat, wagged his head. "Guess you're dead right. Am sort of spooked up. Just don't want anything to happen to that money. Means a lot to me to see that it gets delivered."

Shawn was looking ahead, his eyes sweeping the slopes and ridges now closing in around them.

"Same here," he said absently. "Where's that fork in the road you were telling me about?"

Egan raised himself slightly, considered the road beyond the team. "About three miles farther on," he said, his voice once more taut. "Sure feel better once we're on the Rockville branch. Like I said, there ain't no guarantee, but the chances of us not getting stopped will be some better."

Starbuck nodded his understanding. They were in a fairly wide valley, and the span of blacks were making good time on a slight downgrade. Thick brush lined the shoulders of the road, ran all the way back to the slopes where cedars, piñons, and pines took over. It was ideal country for an ambush.

Shawn felt his pulse quicken. Off to the right, on a ledge midway up the side of the nearby mountain, he had seen motion. Keeping his eyes locked to the point, he saw the head and shoulders of a man appear. Shortly, a second took up a position beside the first. Both were wearing colorless coats of some kind — dusters, probably, although he could not see the men full length and be certain.

The Jenners. There could be no doubt — just as he could be sure the rest of the outlaw gang was somewhere close making preparations to halt the buckboard. He wondered if it was just a routine hold up, or had Jenner been tipped off as to the shipment of bank money?

It didn't matter to Starbuck — it was a situation made to order for him and just what he had hoped for. Twisting about, he raised an arm, drove his fist hard into the jaw of the unsuspecting deputy. He had a quick glimpse of Egan's startled features as he tumbled from the buggy, heard him curse as he struck the ground.

Smiling grimly, Shawn snatched the whip from its socket and, laying it on the blacks, sent them racing down the road.

6

Starbuck flung a hasty glance over his shoulder as the buckboard rocked and whipped from side to side in its wild flight. Troy Egan was lost to sight in the swirling dust, and he could see none of Jenner's men in pursuit as yet. He smiled tautly. He'd gotten the jump on them.

Turning back, he searched the narrowing valley for a place where he could cut off the road. A sharp bend loomed up a quarter mile farther on. If he could reach it, make the turn, he'd be in good shape.

Crouched low, Starbuck plied the whip to the broad backs of the galloping blacks. The curve raced toward him, and he swung around it, leaning far right to keep the buckboard on balance and from capsizing. The vehicle tipped dangerously in spite of his efforts, and for a few breathless moments he thought he was going over, but it righted finally, and the team rushed on.

Ahead, the valley was spreading out once more, with scrubby trees, rabbit brush, oak brush, and the like pushing in from both sides. A small clearing appeared. Unhesitating, he veered the blacks into it, curving them deep into the tangle until he was as far off the road as possible without starting the climb up the slope; then he made a right angle and doubled back into the direction from which he had come.

Pulling the heaving team to a halt, Shawn vaulted over the seat into the bed of the buckboard and yanked the canvas tarp clear of the chest containing the bank's money and supplies. Knocking the padlock clear with the butt of his pistol, he opened it, took out the small cash box. Tucking it under his arm, he wheeled, snatched up the rifle dropped by Troy Egan, and leaped to the ground. A second thought came to him, and taking the sheriff's star from his pocket, he tossed it onto the seat and then, slapping the nearest horse smartly on the rump, sent the team plunging for the road.

He did not wait to see if the blacks, fighting the dense, springy brush while the buckboard bounced and rattled behind them, halted or not. Left to their own, they would reach open ground and eventually return to the road and head back the way they had come.

Moving fast, Shawn struck a direct

course paralleling the route that would lead him to Hackberry. He had no idea how far he was from the settlement. It should be near, he reasoned, judging from what he'd heard; regardless, it would be wise to get as far from the point where he had abandoned the buckboard as quickly as possible. Sid Jenner and his men would have no difficulty in following its wheel tracks after he swung it off the road.

He had covered no more than fifty yards in the heavy brush when the pound of running horses brought him up short. It could be the Egan team, he thought at first, and then discarded the idea when a shout echoed through the quiet.

"Here! Here's where he turned off!"

Hunched low, Starbuck doubled back a few steps to the fringe of the dense growth where he had a better view of the road. There were two riders, both dressed in the customary Jenner gang manner of long, tan-colored dusters and bandanna masks, at the moment pulled down and revealing their faces. Neither man looked familiar.

Shawn watched them walk their horses slowly along the deep imprints left in the soil by the buckboard's wheels, saw them halt abruptly.

"Here's the wagon!" one sang out, and

dismounted immediately.

Four other riders rounded the bend at that moment, galloped forward to join their companions. Starbuck, unable to see all that was taking place, moved farther to his left, gained a position where brush no longer impeded his view. The outlaws were all off the saddle. They had lifted the shipping box from the bed of the buckboard, dumped its contents onto the ground, and were pawing through it.

"The money ain't here," one said finally, straightening up.

"It's supposed to be," the man next to him said, and crouching, began to go through the papers and books once again.

The outlaws had known of the money shipment, Starbuck realized, and gave it thought. Who could have told them about it? Someone in Junction City, of course, and someone close to the men in on the deal — Beasley, Duckworth, Grimshaw, and Troy Egan. . . . Egan. Shawn frowned at the possibility; could it have been the deputy?

Was his apparent nervousness as they drew near the fork in the road where the holdup had apparently been scheduled to take place due to his knowledge that Sid Jenner and his gang were waiting in ambush for them? It was illogical to think that either Duckworth or Beasley would be a party to such a thing, and certainly Charley Grimshaw would not be guilty of stealing his own money and dividing it with the outlaws. And it was just as unlikely they would be so careless as to let word of the shipment being made slip out. It was hard to accept, but Troy Egan was the only —

Starbuck's thoughts came to an abrupt halt. Turlock, the bank's bookkeeper! He'd forgotten about him and there was no doubt he was the most likely possibility of all. He would have had the opportunity and the —

"Spread out!" a voice cut suddenly into Shawn's consideration of the problem. "It's that goddam two-bit sheriff that's took it! He can't have got far!"

Shawn drew back quickly into the deeper brush. The outlaws were splitting up, going three to each side of the road, and in forage line formation were starting to search the thick growth.

Low, moving hurriedly but careful to not disturb the brush, Starbuck began to work his way toward the foot of the slope. If he could reach there, find himself a hiding place in the mass of jumbled rocks and tangled weeds that he could see, he should be able to escape the outlaws, and escape he must. Everything was going just as he'd planned and hoped for, but to let himself be captured now with the money in his possession would not only blow his scheme for getting in with the Jenner gang but probably cost him his life as well.

"What's that moving up ahead?"

Shawn froze. The men were closing in much faster than he had anticipated. Crouched behind a thick clump of oak, he looked back. He could see only one of the outlaws, a hunched shape no more than a dozen steps away.

"Rufe — goddammit, answer me!"

Rufe. . . . That was the name of the man with the drawling Texan, the pair he'd encountered back in Junction City at the swearing-in ceremony. Jenner's men — both of them! He should have suspected it, but he reckoned it didn't matter; it couldn't have worked out better if he'd sent invitations to the outlaws.

"Was just a bird or something."

It was too late to try for the bottom of the slope now. He'd surely be spotted if he continued the attempt; best to lie low where he was, pray that the outlaw nearest him would pass at a safe distance, unnoticing. But if that failed, he could do nothing but shoot down the man, leap onto his horse, and make a run for it.

The muted tunk-a-tunk of the rider's approaching mount grew louder. Starbuck waited tensely, rifle poised, ready to be fired or used as a club, whichever was most practical. Nearby in a sparsely needled piñon a jay hopped from branch to branch, peering at him suspiciously with agate-hard eyes.

"See anything?"

The shouted question came from somewhere along the road. The drawling outlaw close to Starbuck grunted his reply.

"Naw, nothing."

"I'm betting he headed back the other way. . . . How'd it come Jenner figured he'd be in here? He see him?"

"Never said."

Shawn's breathing came to a stop. No more than a wagon's length away the outlaw, a lean shadow on his horse, moved by. He was holding his eyes straight ahead, seemingly having small interest in the search.

"Hell, let's go do some talking to Sid, see if he don't want to look back up the road a piece."

The rider immediately swerved his mount

toward the sound of his friend's voice. "Sure, why not. Sid don't know everything."

Starbuck settled gratefully on his heels as relief ran through him. It had been a tight few minutes, but luck had been with him — would even improve if the men working the brush in his area were able to persuade the outlaw chief to turn the search back to the opposite end of the valley.

Motionless, he rode out time behind the thick clump of oak while the jay continued to observe him; then, finally, he heard the hard rap of hoofs as horses crossed the road. Immediately, he rose and at a slow trot resumed the course that would take him to Hackberry. Shortly, he reached a jutting in the brush and, pausing to look, saw that the outlaws — seven in all — were slowly wending in and out among the trees and scrubby growth at the upper end of the valley.

He grinned in satisfaction. He could forget about Sid Jenner and his men for the time, proceed with his plan. But first it was necessary to rid himself of the cash box containing the bank's money. Glancing about, he located an easily identifiable finger of sandstone extending out from the hillside.

Reaching it and making sure that no one was in the area to witness, he dug a hole and buried the square metal container, taking care to wipe out all traces of freshly turned earth with a leafy branch from a clump of Apache plume.

That done, Shawn again made a painstaking survey of the country, reassured himself that the outlaws were still engaged in beating the brush for him and that there was no one else around to watch. He then continued the hike to Hackberry, hopeful the settlement was not too far distant. Like all men accustomed to living in the saddle, he wasn't much for walking.

7

It was late in the afternoon when Starbuck reached the town. He stood for a time on a low hill that overlooked the settlement, bathed now in the pale amber glow of the receding sun, resting as he studied it carefully and fixed in mind the location and arrangement of its buildings.

As he had been told, Hackberry was small, no more than a half a dozen business structures — several of which appeared to be vacant — and an equal number of houses. All were dominated by a fairly large, two-storied edifice that bore the sign: DOOLEY'S SALOON.

The single street along which the buildings stood in irregular fashion was deserted, and cutting down from the crest of the hill, Shawn crossed and entered the bulky structure. It had been a long, hot walk, and he was hungry and in need of a drink. Too, it was the one place where he could expect to encounter Sid Jenner and his followers.

He was a marked man among both the

law abiding and the lawless now. Like as not, Tony Egan had made it back to Junction City by that hour, and word of the new sheriff's duplicity would already be spreading through the valley. A lawman turned bad — the very worst crime of all to many, the ultimate in treachery, that was the mark he was now wearing. Perhaps details were at that moment being sent to all neighboring towns as well as into adjoining territories and states posting him as a wanted criminal and offering a handsome reward for him — dead or alive.

He grinned tightly at the realization and irony of it. Safety for him lay only in Hackberry now — a town controlled by Sid Jenner, one of the worst outlaws to appear in years — and there only if he played his cards right.

Halting just within the open doorway of the saloon, Starbuck glanced about — a bartender, two garishly dressed women, and no one else. Business was apparently at low ebb. Moving on, aware of the curious glances turned to him by the women, the slightly suspicious stare of the aproned man, Starbuck crossed to the bar.

"Beer," he said, digging into his pocket for a coin. "Be wanting a room later. You the one I talk to about it?"

The bartender set a foam-capped mug before him, picked up the coin. "Reckon I am. Name's Dooley," he said, and added, "Who're you?"

"I'm the man wanting a room," Shawn replied after downing the lukewarm beer. "Can use some grub, too."

Dooley eyed him thoughtfully. "Mister, you know where you are?"

"Dump somebody called Hackberry, but there's some figure it ought to be named Jenner instead."

The saloon man drew up slowly. "You know Sid?"

"Passing acquaintance. . . . What about that room?"

Dooley shrugged. "Upstairs, and it'll be a dollar a night — paid now. Eating's done at them back tables. How long you aiming to stay?"

"Could be for quite a spell," Starbuck said with a wry grin as he laid a silver dollar on the counter, "but I'll take things one at a time. Which room?"

"Any of them on the left-hand side of the hall. Ain't none of them taken. Ones on the right-hand side belong to the girls."

Shawn nodded, turned to the creaky staircase at the end of the counter. Mounting it, he gained a narrow landing

65

and crossed to a shadowy corridor off which a half a dozen doors turned on either side. Halting at the first on his left, he opened the room, glanced in. A rueful smile pulled at his lips.

The room hadn't been cleaned in months, he guessed. The bed was unmade, the covers half on the dusty floor. A broken chair lay in one corner where it had been thrown to rest amid a collection of empty whiskey bottles.

Turning about, he made a tour of the remaining quarters, found all in similar if varying condition. The last in line, however, did appear to be a bit cleaner, and there was water in the china pitcher; he chose it.

Stripping, he washed away the sweat and dust accumulated during the day's activities; then, shaking his clothing vigorously and wiping down the leather vest and flat-crowned hat with a damp cloth, he dressed and returned to the hallway. He could find no key to the room and so placed his rifle under the corn-shuck mattress of the bed where it would escape the eyes of any casual prowler.

There were two customers at the bar, and both turned to have their look at him as he descended the stairs. They were not

Jenner men, he was sure; they appeared rather to be local businessmen. One of the girls arose, crossed to the foot of the steps to meet him. Average size, fairly well built, with yellow-blonde hair. She was not bad-looking.

"I'm Clarissa," she announced with a fixed, glassy smile. "You want to buy me a drink?"

"Later," Starbuck replied. "Right now I'm interested in some grub."

"I can drink while you're eating," Clarissa said, the glassy smile not changing.

"You show me where to go to get it, and you've got yourself a deal."

The girl waved toward the rear of the room. "There, in the back. Front tables are for card playing and drinking, ones against the wall for eating. . . . Find yourself one and I'll tell Joe to bring you out a plateful of the specialty of the house — that's stew."

"Suits me," Shawn said, moving to the nearest table. "Can use some coffee, too."

Clarissa nodded, continued on for a door that led apparently into the kitchen. Starbuck settled down on one of the hard-back chairs, cocked his hat to one side of his head, and swung his attention to the bar. Dooley and the two patrons were in a huddle at the far end of the counter. That he was the topic of conversation was evident by the occasional glances thrown his way.

At that moment Clarissa reappeared, bringing with her a cup of black, steaming coffee. She placed it before him, said, "I'll go get my drink now."

"Sure. Tell Dooley I'll settle with him later."

The girl hesitated. "He won't like that."

Shawn reached into a pocket for a dollar, handed it to her. "This ought to take care of it — and a few more."

Clarissa shrugged, turned away. "I'll be right back."

The kitchen door opened, and an elderly man wearing a stained apron came into the room carrying Starbuck's meal. Wordless, he set the deep plate on the table, laid a knife, fork and spoon beside it, and retreated.

Shawn took up the fork, studied the food. It was a combination of potatoes, beef chunks, beans, and some other vegetable. The meat was leathery, the rest old and no doubt withered when introduced into the stew pot, but he began to eat at once, nevertheless, a hungry man in need of sustenance.

Clarissa rejoined him, taking the chair opposite. She had a near-full bottle of whiskey and, placing it in the center of the table with two glasses, said, "If we drink it all, you owe Dooley another dollar."

Starbuck continued to eat. More patrons entered the saloon, but they, too, appeared to be local residents and not Jenner men. He was certain the outlaws would show up, but just when was a question. Dooley's was their hangout while in Hackberry, and undoubtedly they were the saloon's chief support.

He felt Clarissa's eyes drilling into him, glanced up. "You wanting to ask a question?"

She smiled, then looked away. "Maybe. All those fancy clothes you're wearing — they look new."

"Could be they are," Shawn replied, finishing the meal and pushing the plate aside.

The girl nodded, picked up the bottle of liquor, and filled his glass. "Wondering, too, what you're doing here. You don't look like the kind."

"Kind? What kind?"

"Somebody dodging the law."

Starbuck took a swallow of the raw whiskey, leaned back in his chair. "Reckon you can't go by looks, then, because that's what brought me here. Heard this was a town where a man didn't have to worry about badge toters."

"No, only Sid Jenner," she murmured.

"Jenner. . . . I've heard of him, too."

Clarissa shrugged, pushed a stray lock of hair back from her face, sipped at her drink. "Could say he runs this town — him and his bunch."

"A real genuine ringtail, eh? Expect I ought to meet him, get acquainted."

"You will," Clarissa said lazily. "Makes it his business to know all about everybody that comes through here, especially the ones that don't keep on going."

Starbuck smiled. Sid Jenner was a lot more anxious to meet him than the girl could suspect. He shifted his attention to the bar. Dooley's patrons had increased to an even half dozen, and two more heavily rouged and gaudily clad women were now present, mingling with the customers lined up at the counter.

"Was hoping you were just riding through."

Shawn came back to the girl. "That so?"

She leaned forward, elbows on the table, eyes serious and intent. "I want to get out of this town. Thought I might go with you when you left."

70

"Sort of planned on staying a spell. Stage goes through here — other pilgrims, too. Why don't you just line up and leave?"

Clarissa shook her head. "Sid Jenner won't let me."

"You his woman?"

"Was — not anymore."

"Then why don't you pull out?"

"Sid passed the word that I'm not to leave. None of the stage drivers will let me get aboard, and if I try to go with some cowhand or other pilgrim, Dooley or maybe another of the town's good citizens warns them to stay clear of me or expect a bullet."

"Then what makes you think I can get you out of here?"

Clarissa smiled faintly. "Not sure. Just something about you, something that sort of stirred up the hope inside me. . . . Will — will you help me?"

"Would like to for sure," Starbuck replied after a long silence. "Only thing is I —"

His voice trailed off. Two men had come through the saloon's doorway, were crossing to the bar. Shawn drew up slowly. One was Rufe, the other the outlaw who had so closely passed him by during the search in the brush. Jenner men. . . . Now it would all begin in earnest.

71

8

Clarissa's expression had changed to one of weary resignation. "Guess I was wrong," she said heavily, and turned to follow Starbuck's gaze. "They're part of the Jenner bunch. One with the two guns is Rufe Gorman. Other one is Saul Tinker."

Shawn watched the pair swagger up to the counter, take a position at its near end. Rufe brushed at his mustache.

"Give us a bottle, Dooley, and be goddam quick about it."

The bartender hastened to comply, obviously hopeful of pacifying the outlaw's apparent ill humor.

"The whole outfit usually come to town together?"

"Not always," Clarissa said, refilling her glass. "What makes you so interested in them?"

"Just wondering," Starbuck replied with a shrug.

"Not a healthy thing to do around here. Folks steer clear of them if they want to stay alive."

"Seems you had plenty to do with them once and you're still living."

"Barely," Clarissa said in a rueful voice. "Not sure why I am, either. Probably because there's a shortage around — shortage of women."

"Why won't Jenner let you leave?"

"Know too much. Know where the hideout is, and I know who's in the gang. He's afraid I'll talk if I ever get out of here."

"Hideout?" Starbuck echoed absently, toying with his glass. "Figured they'd be staying right here in town."

"No, Sid's smarter than that." The girl hesitated. "You telling me the truth about not knowing him and the others? Rufe and Saul are giving you the once-over."

Shawn did not raise his head, simply looked up through his brows. The outlaws were staring at him fixedly.

"Guess maybe we did sort of meet —"

"It's him!" Rufe Gorman suddenly yelled, drawing his pistol. "By God, it's him!"

Tinker appeared uncertain. "You sure?"

"I am," Rufe snapped. "Ain't no missing that black hat — and that vest. Got a look at him from the hill when he went driving by."

Silence had fallen over the saloon, and Shawn felt all eyes turned upon him. Deliberate, he refilled his glass from the

73

bottle, took a slow sip. Saul Tinker was still unsure, probably finding it hard to believe that a man who had hijacked a shipment of money out from under Sid Jenner and his followers would be so bold, or foolish, as to show up in the outlaws' town.

"You reckon we ought to go get Sid?"

"Can take care of it myself," Gorman answered, and pulling away from the bar, moved up to Starbuck's table. Shawn continued to look down.

"You — Sheriff!" Rufe barked harshly.

Starbuck glanced up. "Talking to me?"

"You're goddam right I am! Was a pretty cute stunt you pulled, knocking out that deputy and taking off with the money."

"I figured it was," Shawn said blandly.

"Well, you sure made a big mistake coming here to hide! Picked the wrong town."

"That so? Always heard it was the right one."

The patrons at the bar with Dooley had drawn nearer, were watching and listening intently. It was growing darker in the big room, and a swamper had appeared and was beginning to light the oil lamps placed about on the walls. He, too, had paused to look on.

"Get up," Gorman ordered suddenly. "We're taking you to see Sid."

Starbuck screwed his chair about noisily

to where he could face the outlaws. "No, reckon not. Like it right here. This Sid wants to see me, you bring him in."

Gorman swore, jammed his pistol into its holster, and reached for Starbuck. Shawn came up fast, jabbed a left fist into the man's face, crossed with a hard right. As Rufe staggered back, Starbuck drew his weapon, leveled it at Tinker.

Rufe, blind mad, whirled and lunged. Shawn caught him a solid blow across the temple with his gun. The outlaw wilted, began to fall forward. Catching him with the palm of his free hand, Starbuck shoved him roughly into Saul Tinker.

"Get him out of here before he gets himself hurt," he said quietly.

Saul caught Gorman around the waist, supported his sagging body. His face was red with anger.

"You know what you're doing, mister?"

"Reckon so," Shawn answered, holstering his weapon. "I need to make it plainer to you?"

Tinker swore deeply and, draping one of Rufe's arms about his neck, started to wheel.

"We'll be coming back," he warned, moving toward the doorway with the sagging body of Gorman slack against him. "And Sid'll be with us."

"Find me easy," Starbuck said, smiling at Clarissa as he resumed his chair. "Like the company, so I'll be right here."

Dooley, features taut, watched Tinker half drag, half carry Gorman from the room and then crossed stiffly to where Starbuck sat.

"I want no trouble with Jenner," he said angrily. "You figure to buck him, go somewheres else to do it."

"Not figuring anything," Shawn said coolly. "Seems it's him that's got something on his mind."

"Makes no difference which way it is, I don't want him and his bunch down on me. I leave them alone, and they do the same for me. Same goes for the whole town."

"So? What've I got to do with it?"

"Rufe said something about you being a sheriff."

"Was," Starbuck corrected pointedly. "Saw a chance to better myself and took it. . . . Don't fret about me and the Jenners. I'm not aiming to mess up your deal."

The arrangement between the outlaws and Hackberry was a delicately balanced affair, it appeared; each protected the other for his own sake, like rival bull elks surrounded by hungry wolves awaiting only an opportunity to close in.

Dooley shook his head, glanced at the men at the bar behind him. "Well, want it understood. You've been warned. Aim to tell Jenner that."

"Tell him what you like," Starbuck said indifferently. "Man means nothing to me."

The saloonkeeper turned away, resumed his customary place behind the counter. Clarissa leaned forward again, a strange light in her eyes.

"What Rufe said true? Did you beat Sid Jenner out of some money?"

"Don't know as I beat him out of anything that was his. Money was a shipment I was taking to the bank in Rockville. Figured I needed it worse than they did. If he had the same idea, he come just a little late. About all I can do about it is say I'm sorry."

"Unless you're mighty good or mighty careful," the girl said slowly, "you'll be more than sorry. You'll be dead."

"Maybe."

"If you've got the money on you, best thing you can —"

Shawn interrupted her with, "I don't. Hid it back up the way."

A smile spread slowly across the girl's lips as understanding came to her. "Well, do tell!" she murmured. "Looks like some-body's finally come along and got the best of Sid Jenner. What's the game?"

"Game? No game. It's my money. I grabbed it and intend to keep it. Turned my back on a good job doing it and made myself an outcast far as the rest of the country goes. After paying that kind of a price, I intend to enjoy every nickel of it. Sure don't aim to hand it over to some-body named Jenner."

"And you came here so's you could lay low —"

"From what I'd heard it's the best place I could pick."

"Far as the outside's concerned. Not so sure about Sid Jenner, though. He's not going to let you get away with it, so don't sell him short. He's smart, and he's maybe the meanest man in the world along with it. Won't hold off a second from putting a bullet in your head."

"He will long as he doesn't know where that money's hid, and I'm not about to tell him. Doubt if he's as interested in killing me as he is in getting his hands on it."

Clarissa filled her glass, nodded. "You're holding the best cards now, all right," she said, lifting her drink in salute. "Here's to your luck not running out. . . . Obliged to you for the whiskey," she finished.

"Been my pleasure," Starbuck replied, rising with her. "Think I'll have a look-see at the town before I turn in."

Concern filled the girl's eyes. "I — I wouldn't if I were you. Rufe Gorman could still be hanging around, and after the way you handled him, he'll probably be of a mind to shoot you first, tell Jenner later."

Starbuck glanced about the room. The same patrons were there, and no new ones had entered. The swamper had completed lighting the lamps, even the big wagon-wheel chandelier that hung by a rope from the ceiling, and was now engaged in re-arranging some of the chairs.

"Possible," Shawn said, "but if this Jenner's the hell bender folks keep saying he is, I doubt if any of his bunch do anything without first asking. . . . When does the stage go through here?"

She looked at him in surprise. "North-bound on Friday, the southbound on Saturday. Doesn't stop unless there's a passenger getting on."

"Where's the regular stations?"

"Junction City north, Jonesboro south. Why? You thinking about taking it?"

"Just might — someday," Starbuck said, and strolled toward the doorway.

9

Shawn was up early that next morning, and after a breakfast of paper-dry fried eggs, salt pork, bread, and coffee, made his way to the porch fronting Dooley's.

Hackberry, what there was of it, lay in absolute quiet, the few firms still stocked to do business not yet open to handle the needs of any customers who might present themselves. He ticked them off idly: a grocery store, a gun and saddle shop, a livery stable, and of course, Dooley's. There was nothing else. The town was as near dead as it could be, managing survival on the strength of the Jenner gang's patronage and by feeding upon itself.

It was sad that Hackberry, so studiously avoided by the outside world because of the outlaws, was in a state of suspension. It would be a fine place to live, situated as it was in the lower mountains, with grass-covered slopes and flats, tall pines, and their smaller counterparts, the cedars, junipers, and piñons abundant everywhere.

Bright flowers carpeted the sinks, and

game was plentiful; he had seen mule deer, wild turkeys, quail, rabbits, as well as a flock of ducks sporting about on a pond not far from the settlement.

Like as not it seldom got too hot or too cold in the surrounding valley, and the stream he had noted, fed by snow banks farther north in the higher Colorado mountains, probably would never sink too low to supply everyone's needs.

It would be ideal country in which to settle down, raise cattle or horses, have a family, and know the deep satisfaction of having a home, Starbuck thought as he stared out over the land, soft-edged in the early-morning light. A man could find all the answers he sought there. Only it was not for him, at least it could not be until he found Ben. When that was done and all pending matters cleared up, then he could think about his own needs and desires.

Shawn drew to attention, his mind abruptly washing itself clean of all such consideration. A half a dozen or so riders had entered the street from its north end. He spotted Gorman and Saul Tinker at once, knew immediately that it was Sid Jenner and his guns, that they were coming for him.

Cool, he leaned against one of the

81

squared timbers that served as support for the roof of Dooley's porch and watched them pull up to the hitchrack. There was a raw, red lump on the side of Gorman's head, and the tall Texan with the drawling voice had supplied himself with a new hat. The man in the center of the party, a big, thick-shouldered, bearded redhead with small dark eyes and a slash for a mouth, was undoubtedly Sid Jenner. Silent, he watched them dismount, tie their horses, and step up onto the porch.

Jenner halted in front of Starbuck, stared at him coldly. His followers formed a half circle behind him.

"Inside —"

Shawn's shoulder stirred slightly. "Just came out. Reckon I'll stay — air's fresher."

Gorman muttered an oath. Jenner's ruddy face darkened. "Don't wise off with me, mister! Best you don't get yourself in any more trouble than you are."

"Don't see as I am — not with you, anyway," Starbuck said easily.

Sid Jenner's eyes narrowed. "The hell you're not!" he snarled, and made a motion with his hand. "Reo — Jubal, bring him inside!"

Guns drawn, two of the men moved up to Starbuck. Each caught him by an arm,

pulled him about, the older of the pair re-
lieving him of his gun as he did, and
pushed him in behind the outlaw leader,
now passing through the doorway. There
was no conversation between the men as
they followed, only a deep, almost sullen
silence.

Jenner staked to the far side of the saloon, ignoring Dooley who stood at the
end of the bar frowning anxiously. Jerking
out one of the chairs, he settled onto it,
kicked the one opposite from the table,
and bucked his head at Shawn.

"Set there."

Reo and Jubal did not wait for Starbuck
to comply of his own accord, simply
shoved him roughly onto the seat and
stepped back. Gorman, the Texan, Saul
Tinker, and the one whose name he had
not yet heard called moved in beside them.

"Where's the money?"

Jenner came directly to the point.
Starbuck studied the man in silence. He
must move carefully, he knew, to accomplish
what he had planned, but his life depended
on the box he had cached back along the
road. As long as he could keep it from Sid
Jenner and his bunch, he would stay alive; it
was a solitary thin wall standing between
him and failure — and death.

"Don't see as that's any business of yours."

Jenner's jaw tightened, and again Rufe Gorman swore in a strangled sort of way.

"See how he's acting, Sid?" he shouted. "Like he done yesterday — smarting off and —"

"Everything around here's my business," Jenner said harshly, ignoring Rufe. "Sooner you get that in your head the better off you'll be!"

Starbuck managed a half smile as he fought to maintain an attitude of indifference. "Still don't see what all this's got to do with me."

"That box of cash you took yesterday, it's mine."

"Yours? You got it wrong. Belonged to the bank in Junction City."

"I was waiting for it. You crossed me up. Now I aim to have it."

Shawn stirred lazily. The faces of the men standing behind the outlaw chief were taut, angry, and he could see that Sid Jenner was controlling his temper with difficulty.

"Way I see it, thing like this it's first come, first served. Maybe you figured to grab that money for yourself, but you missed out. I beat you to it, and I'm hanging on to it."

"The hell you are," the Texan said in a

low voice. "Reckon it's us that calls the tune around here."

Several others joined in a chorus of agreement. Jenner studied Starbuck thoughtfully. Then, "There's ways to make you talk."

"Sweat it out of me, that it? Use some Apache tricks? Be a waste of time. Never had that much money before in my life, probably won't ever get the chance to get it again. Means you'll have to kill me, and if you do that, nobody'll ever find the box."

"I can make him do some yakking, Sid. Just you turn me loose on him."

It was the one Jenner had called Jubal, a squat, dark, hard case with a scar on the left side of his face. Likely once an Indian scout, Shawn decided, and well versed in all of the tribal tortures.

Again Jenner was silent for a time. Finally, "No, don't think we'd get anywhere that way. He's fool enough to let you kill him before speaking up."

"Then how the hell you aim —"

"Starbuck — that your name?" Jenner continued, leaning forward.

"Expect you know it is. Been told nothing goes on in this part of the country that you don't see or hear about."

Jenner's rows lifted, expressing his pride

in the fact. "That's right. It's what keeps me on top. Now, if you heard that, you probably know this is my private stomping grounds, and nobody horns in on it. Reason why I'm not letting you get away with hijacking me."

Shawn smiled thinly. "Seems I am."

"Maybe you think you are," Jenner snapped, "but you're fooling yourself."

"Long as I've got the money and you haven't, I'd say it was me on top."

"Like I said, you're fooling yourself, but I'm willing to talk turkey with you, something I don't bother to do very often."

"Guess that's supposed to please me."

Sid Jenner passed up the dry comment. "Been told you're a lawman — or was till you took off with that money. Means every badge in the territory'll be hunting you. Same goes for the rest of the country. Lawmen purely hate a man that's pulled that. Seem to take it personal.

"Now, while you're with me, you're safe. Law gets nowhere around here because I'm the law. Now, you fork over that cash box and I'll forget what you've done to me and let you join up with my outfit. You'll start drawing your share of the take same as the others."

Starbuck let his glance run over the

members of Sid Jenner's gang. For men who were a part of an organized, successful bank of outlaws, all, except for Sid Jenner himself, appeared to be far from prosperous. Their clothing was faded, worn, and in need of replacement; boots were ragged and run-down, and their hats, except for the new one being worn by Tex, had long since seen better days. None looked to have shaved or even washed in months, and their eyes reflected a life of endless quarreling and dissipation.

"How much'll my share be?" Shawn asked, curious.

"I take half of what we get because it's me that has all the connections and does all the figuring. Other half's split six ways — seven when you throw in with us."

Starbuck shrugged. "Not much of a deal — when all I have to do is keep my mouth shut and have it all."

"Maybe so, but the only thing is you'll find it plenty hard to enjoy any of it, penned up like you'll be."

"Penned up?"

"What I said — penned up and living like a dog in a cage I'll fix for you."

10

Starbuck allowed the outlaw's threat to have its effect on him. He was being careful not to capitulate too readily to Sid Jenner's demands but knew it would be a mistake to let the matter go too far. Caged, or in some other manner restricted and unable to move about freely, it would be impossible to further pursue his plan, which was working much better so far than he had hoped.

"Maybe we ought to find us a mangy old flea-bit hound to put in there with him," the man called Reo suggested.

"One of Maria's goats'd be better," Jubal said. "They'd stink a polecat off a gut wagon."

All but Jenner laughed. He continued to study Shawn with his small, hard-surfaced eyes.

"Not looking for something like that," Starbuck murmured, shaking his head and frowning.

"Didn't figure you'd be, but that's how it'll wind up unless you come to time."

"Still don't figure I'm getting a square

deal. Dues to join up with your outfit's a bit high. There's close to eight thousand dollars in that box —"

"Seventy-five hundred," Jenner corrected.

Shawn nodded. The outlaw had inside information; that was certain now. It could hardly be anyone but Turlock, the bank's bookkeeper.

"All right, seventy-five hundred. Giving all that up for a one-seventh share in half is plenty steep."

"Maybe, but you take a look at what you'll be getting. Main thing, the law won't ever bother you none — not long as you run with me. And you'll be getting paid off right along, every time we make a raid. Won't take long to make up what it's costing you."

"Could be quite a while."

Jenner settled back in his chair. "Well, that's what your dues, as you call 'em, will be. You ain't got a choice, anyway. You walked yourself right into a trap when you showed up here, which sure was mighty dumb. Now that you're in it, you just as well come across and make it easy on yourself."

"Could pull out —"

"And ride straight into one of them posses that's working the whole country for you? Forget it. There's two things you can do — turn that cash over to me and throw in with us, or get yourself put in that cage I was telling you about, which'll all end up the same. Either way I'll get the money."

"Might as well own up to it, Dude," Tex said. "We got you by the short hair."

Shawn stirred. "Like to do some thinking on it."

"What's to think about?" Gorman demanded angrily. "Like Sid said, you ain't got no choice. Either you hand over the money, or we'll make you hand it over!"

Jenner raised his hand for silence, his gaze locked to Starbuck's features. "Could be that's a good idea," he said slowly. "You're plenty sure of yourself, and that's set me to wondering."

"Wondering about what?" Rufe asked irritably.

Alarm was flooding through Shawn. Had he overplayed his hand? Had he aroused suspicions within the outlaw leader by being too sure of himself?

"Seems to me he's a mite cool about things. He knows he don't have a chance, yet he sets there trying to bargain like he's got a black ace in the hole."

"You mean he maybe ain't what he's claiming to be?"

"Something like that —"

"But I seen him up in Junction City!" Gorman protested. "So did Kinkaid. We was there watching when they hung the star on him, made him sheriff."

"And we seen him kick that deputy off the wagon and hightail it with the money," Reo said. "Just don't see how you figure he could be flimflamming us."

"Maybe it's all a put-up job so we'll let him throw in with us," Jenner said quietly.

A heavy silence followed the outlaw leader's words. Shawn felt the hard, pushing stares of the men. His life wasn't worth a plugged copper, he realized, if he failed to convince them.

"Couple of things I'm puzzling about," Jenner said. "For one, why'd you wait so long to dump the deputy? You do that for show — specially for us?"

Starbuck managed a smile. "Had figured to do it when we got closer to Rockville, but I spotted you waiting and decided if I was going to get my hands on the money, I'd have to do it before you hit us. So I got rid of him and made a run for it."

"Sure didn't run far," Kinkaid, the drawling Texan, observed dryly.

"With three of you on my tail right quick?" Shawn said impatiently. "Hell, only thing I could do was duck into the brush and lay low until you quit looking for me."

"That where you hid the cash box — there where you turned off the road?" Jenner asked slyly.

"No, was on a ways."

"Why'd you come here?" Gorman pressed. "Don't go trying to make me believe you didn't know this was our town. You was shooting off your mouth about it back there in Junction City."

"No place close but Hackberry, and I was afoot. Only choice I had. . . . Was the reason I'd planned it all to happen closer to Rockville."

Sid Jenner shrugged. "Well, could be what you're telling us is straight, but I'm not banking on it. Just don't believe in taking chances on something like this when there ain't no need."

Starbuck breathed easier. He'd gotten through the worst part; Jenner appeared to be more or less satisfied, and his decision, regardless of how the others felt, was what would count.

"Then what're you going to do?" Reo asked. "Put him in that pen you was talking about until we're for sure?"

"Just what I don't want to do, take him

to the camp," Jenner said, shaking his head. "If he's some kind of a lawman, that's what he's after — getting us to show him where it is so's he can somehow slip off later and bring back a posse."

"Godalmighty!" Gorman exploded. "You ain't going to just let him run loose around here, are you?"

"Why not? Where can he go? If he's telling us the truth, he sure won't risk sticking his nose out of Hackberry, not with every lawman and john citizen prowling the country ready to shoot him on sight.

"And if he ain't, what can he do? The law — even the army — has been here before and didn't find nothing, so bringing them here won't mean anything. . . . But I don't aim to leave any gates open. We'll keep an eye on him while I do some looking into things."

Shawn smiled, made a show of indifference. "Suit yourself."

He was feeling much better. He hadn't gone too far, after all, had only delayed matters for another day or so. Let Sid Jenner go ahead and do his investigating; he had taken great pains to cover his tracks.

"What things you talking about?"

"Junction City — and him being the sheriff."

Rufe Gorman swore. "Told you me and Kinkaid seen them pin the badge on him!"

"Know that, and I'm not doubting you. What I want to find out is whether it was on the level."

"You mean maybe it was all for show —"

"That's what I said before and what I mean."

"How you going to prove it, one way or the other?"

"Easy. Want a couple of you to take a ride up to Junction City, see just what it's like there. If things are sort of quiet like, then I think we can figure this jasper is a ringer. But if everybody's riled up, hollering about lynching and such — and I mean everybody, not just the bigwigs — we can be sure he done what he claims he did — double-crossed them and stole the money."

Gorman bobbed his understanding. "Me and Kinkaid'll get started right away."

"No, you two've been there, and folks'll remember you. Could start them thinking."

"I'll go," Reo said. "Me and Monte. Ain't nobody there ever seen us."

Monte was the name of the sixth outlaw. He was a husky, sullen-looking man with pale-blue eyes that contrasted

94

oddly with his dark features.

"All right, it's your job. Just remember — don't do much talking, just listening. Man asks too many questions will set others to wondering."

Gorman hawked, spat into a nearby cuspidor. "Sure wish't it was me going," he said absently. "Drinking whiskey's a lot better there than in this joint. . . . You want Monte and Reo to bring back your horse?" he added suddenly, turning his attention to Starbuck. "I recollect he was a mighty fine animal."

Shawn saw Jenner's eyes narrow slightly as he waited to hear the answer. "Sure would like to have that sorrel," he said coolly, "but I reckon not. Somebody might spot them taking him and follow, and I don't want a posse breathing down my neck. Just have to fall back on your string."

Jenner nodded. "We got plenty of stock. Wouldn't want you riding a horse folks'd remember, anyway."

He would appreciate having the sorrel — a big, strong gelding that he knew well and could rely on under any and all circumstances — and the impulse to accept Rufe Gorman's suggestion had been tempting and almost tripped him up. But he had thought fast enough to decline, pointing out the obvious danger, and by so doing had moved a step further into Jenner's confidence.

The outlaw chief shifted on his chair, motioned to Dooley. The bar owner came forward at once, bringing with him a full bottle of whiskey and a handful of shot glasses. Setting all on the table, he wheeled, hurried away.

Jenner poured himself a drink, shoved the container at the nearest man. "The boys'll be back tomorrow sometime," he said to Starbuck. "You just sit quiet. If everything turns out all right, you're in with us."

The bottle was making the rounds. Shawn reached up, calmly intercepted it. Filling his own glass, he passed it back over his shoulder, not troubling to look. There was a muttered curse from someone behind him, but he did not miss the faint smile that pulled at Sid Jenner's lips.

"That'll give me time to do some deciding," he said.

"Only deciding you have to do," Jenner stated in a flat voice, "is whether you're going to tell me where you hid that money first off or after you've sweated out a couple of weeks in a dog pen!"

"Yep, we'll see which," Starbuck said indifferently as Jenner got to his feet. "Main thing, don't forget to send me a horse. No hand at riding double."

11

The next day began slowly. Starbuck, rising early from habit, spent the morning hours in Dooley's place and in wandering about the town. That he was being watched was evident. Twice he caught sight of riders on the hill that overlooked Hackberry and realized that for all the confidence displayed by Sid Jenner, the outlaw chief had issued orders to keep tabs on him.

The noon meal was eaten in a small grove of trees across the street from the saloon and in the company of Clarissa who somehow managed a basket of sandwiches, canned peaches for dessert, and coffee. The girl was disturbed by what lay ahead for him. He saw that at once and endeavored to quiet her fears by assuring her that Jenner would do nothing drastic as long as he was unable to get his hands on the bank money, safely cached in the hills.

"You think you can buy yourself a partnership with Sid by handing it over to him?" she asked.

"It's a thought," Shawn replied noncommittally.

Clarissa shook her head. "You wouldn't be a partner for long — just until he could find the right moment to put a bullet in your back. You'd show more sense to get your money and leave."

Shawn gestured toward the hilltop. "Wouldn't get far, not with them up there watching."

He was sitting with his back against a tree trunk. She leaned toward him, laid a hand on his arm. "If I could show you a way, how we could get horses and slip by them without being seen, would you be willing to try?"

Starbuck stirred uncomfortably. The appeal in the girl's voice was strong, and there was hope in her eyes.

"I couldn't do it alone because it would take a man to handle the hostler at the livery stable. We'd have to force him to give us horses, and you could do that."

"Afraid I'm being looked after too close for that."

She withdrew her hand slowly. "I see."

He wished he could tell her his real reason for being unable to help, but too much depended upon his being admitted into the outlaw gang and thereby learning the location of their so carefully concealed hideout.

"Maybe later," he said.

Clarissa smiled wanly. "It doesn't really matter, I guess. I suppose if I were someone else, not what I am —"

"Has nothing to do with it."

"Then why?"

It had become a dangerous topic to be discussing, and he was anxious to get off it. The girl, according to what she had said, had no love for Sid Jenner, but that could or could not be true. The outlaw was a sly and clever man, and it was entirely possible she was planted there in Dooley's saloon for just such a purpose.

He had a moment's wonder about her and Jenner. Both appeared to be a cut above those they associated with, and it would seem natural for them to be together. Once she had been his woman, she'd said; had they come there together, later ostensibly parted company so that Jenner might better perform his operation, or had they truly separated, become the enemies the girl professed?

It was a question Shawn knew he could not answer, and to become involved was far too risky. But later, if all went well, and she was sincere in her wish to leave Hackberry and seek another life, he would see to it that it came to pass. Meanwhile, he had no choice but to regard her in the same light as the rest of Sid Jenner's outlaws.

"You haven't answered —"

The hammer of hoofs as horses swung into the street from beyond the livery stable cut into her question. It was the Texan, Kinkaid, and Saul Tinker. With a spare mount in tow they pulled up at the rack in front of Dooley's. Without leaving the saddle, Kinkaid faced the saloon's open doorway and shouted.

"Starbuck!"

Shawn got to his feet, took up the basket the girl had brought, and helped her rise. "Here," he answered as they crossed the street.

The Texan turned to him. "Sid's wanting you. Let's go."

Starbuck nodded. "Got to get my rifle," he said, taking Clarissa by the elbow and assisting her up the steps.

"Hell with it — come on!"

Starbuck calmly ignored the order, continued on. Entering the saloon, he passed the basket with its cups and leftovers to the girl.

"Obliged to you for everything," he said, smiling.

She nodded woodenly. "I — I wish you wouldn't do —" she began, and then, shrugging, let the words die.

"Don't worry, I'll be back," he said, and climbing the stairs, went to his room and recovered the weapon hidden under the bed's mattress. Hanging it in the crook of an elbow, he returned to the steps and descended. Both Kinkaid and Tinker, features angry, were waiting near the bar for him. The big Texan shook a warning finger at him.

"By God, next time I tell you something, you'd best —"

"Next time, don't!" Starbuck snarled. "Be a waste of breath. I don't take orders from anybody."

Ignoring the pair, he walked on to the door, crossed to the hitchrack, and mounted the bay Jenner had provided for him. Moments later, the two outlaws, jaws set, joined him, and together all three rode out of town.

They swung due west beyond the livery barn, across open country, following no marked trail and pointing generally for a range of rugged mountains ten or twelve miles in the distance. Silence hung between them, and while Shawn was anxious to learn what Reo and Monte had found to be the situation in Junction City, he did not ask. It would be smart to maintain a show of indifference and thus point up his complete confidence.

As they rode, Shawn took careful note of the route being followed, getting the lay of the land and establishing major landmarks in his mind. A time later they left the flats, reached low, broken foothills, and began to veer north toward an irregular ribbon of buttes. The country was mostly barren except for globular clumps of snakeweed, beds of prickly pear, and an occasional cholla cactus, but when they reached the bluffs, small cedars began to appear.

They climbed to the top of the buttes, the mountains now looming darkly before them, crossed a grassy plain, and dropped into a narrow arroyo that widened gradually as they drew nearer to the pine-covered slopes of the high hills.

Shortly, they cut off into a canyon coming in at a right angle, and Starbuck's attention was drawn to a small adobe hut squatting on its far side. Smoke was drifting upward from its chimney, a dozen or so goats grazed on the scanty grass surrounding the place, while a flock of chickens scratched in the dust of a brush-enclosed yard.

This could not be the outlaw camp, Starbuck knew, looking it over curiously as they drew abreast. A woman, Mexican undoubtedly, well up in years and fat to the point of finding difficulty in walking, appeared in the low doorway and waddled into the open. A wide smile cracked her dark face. She waved in recognition, then, turning, re-entered the hut. She would be the Maria the outlaws had spoken of — Maria and her goats.

They moved on into the deepening canyon. It occurred to Shawn that the hut stood at the mouth of the cleavage. At such a location, and assuming the hideout was ahead, old Maria was in an ideal position to warn Sid Jenner and his guns of the approach of a posse or anyone else searching for them. If true, it was small wonder all attempts to track down the gang had failed; in such broken, wild country and with a guard on duty at all times it would be a near impossibility to find the outlaws' base.

A quarter hour later they swung up out of the canyon onto a small flat. A half a dozen rotting gray shacks stood at the base of a towering cliff at its lower end. Several dark holes in the rock marked mine-shaft entrances. They were at an abandoned mining camp, but there were no signs of Sid Jenner and the others.

Wondering, Starbuck continued on with his two sullen guides, moving with them through the decaying structures until they were near the face of the cliff, at which point the trail they followed would necessarily end. Surprise rolled through Shawn when instead of being forced to halt, Tinker spurred his horse into the tall brush and shouldered his way through it to a second plateau. Following the outlaw into the clearing, Starbuck saw a second scatter of shacks, all in considerably better condition than the first group, while in the face of the cliff there was but one shaft opening. As he glanced at it, two men stepped out into view. One was Sid Jenner, the other Rufe Gorman.

They had reached the hideout, and it became even clearer to Shawn why no one had ever found it. Should anyone get by old Maria and come to the first of the deserted mining camps, they would assume the trail entered there, never being aware of a second camp on the hidden, lower level.

"Head over to that barn," Kinkaid said, pointing to one of the larger structures.

Starbuck, eyes taking in the details of the area in a swift survey, obediently swung his horse toward the indicated building. The outlaws rode close to him on either side, and when they came to the improvised door that filled an opening in one wall, all halted. Tinker dropped from his saddle, freed the loop of rope that served as a latch.

"Climb down," the Texan ordered.

Starbuck swung off the bay and came about. Tinker, in charge of the horses, led them into the building in which Shawn could see several other mounts.

"He give you any trouble?"

The question came from Jenner, moving up with Rufe at his side. Beyond them Jubal and the man called Monte, with two sleazy-looking women, had come from the mine shaft and were now lounging against the face of the cliff.

"Nope, sure didn't," Kinkaid replied.

"Reckon there was no reason for him to," the outlaw chief said.

Starbuck smiled. "Guess you found out what you wanted to know."

"I did. There's a thousand-dollar reward waiting for anybody that brings you in, dead or alive. Whole town's squalling for your hide on account of the way you took them in, let them make you the sheriff, then used the job to get away with all that money."

The groundwork he had laid in Junction City had paid off well. All, including Beasley, John Duckworth, and Deputy Troy Egan, believed him to now be a criminal, a presumption he had taken pains to create, fearing that without it the odds for convincing Sid Jenner of his sincerity would be hopeless.

"Posses out looking for me?" he asked, putting a note of pride in his tone.

"Reo said the country was crawling with them. They got stopped twice."

Gorman grinned. "And they got orders to shoot you on sight. . . . Mister, you ain't got the chance of a dogie at a sheepherder's barbecue if you ever poke your snout out of this valley!"

Reo, with Saul Tinker and Kinkaid, had now joined the group. Monte and Jubal still dallied at the mine-shaft entrance. Living quarters evidently were maintained inside.

"Wasn't planning on it," Shawn said.

Jenner nodded coldly. "You're being smart. . . . Where's the money hid?"

12

Starbuck shrugged. He had successfully maneuvered his way into the outlaws' hideout, now came the task of getting out — alive. He could look for no help, of course, from the posses roaming the hills and flats in search of him; they would listen to no explanations, which was as he expected it to be.

His solitary source of aid now was U.S. Marshal Bill Granett at the capitol in Santa Fe to whom he'd outlined his plans at the very beginning and who was expecting to hear from him.

"Can't tell you that," he said.

Jenner's face flushed brightly. "What the hell's that mean?" he demanded angrily.

"Just plain don't know exactly where it is. Country's all new to me. Have to go down there, get my bearings."

Reo, a heavily built, hard-set gunman with flat, gray eyes, studied Shawn coldly. "Going to be somewheres along the road after you wheeled off that buckboard."

"Yeh, know that, but I kept walking for quite a ways. Remember climbing a slope and coming out onto a little meadow, or maybe it was before that. Seems there was a rock slide —"

"Goddammit, he's horsing us around!" Rufe Gorman shouted abruptly. "I'm for taking him and —"

"No, guess it was a big pile of boulders," Shawn finished. "But come to think of it, wouldn't be too smart for me to go poking around down there now, not with half the territory hunting me. I get shot out of the saddle or roped in, everybody'll be out of luck."

Gorman swore again, but Jenner nodded thoughtfully. "Some sense to what you're saying."

Jubal, finally deciding to join the meeting, moved up at that moment. "What's going on?"

"This goddam joker claims he don't recollect where he buried that money, and he's scared to go looking for it on account of them posses!" Gorman stormed. "I say we ought to —"

"We'll wait," Jenner cut in harshly. "If you had a lick of sense in that thing you call a head, you'd know he was right."

Gorman drew up stiffly. "Best you ease off there a bit, Sid. You ain't talking to no flunky."

"I'm telling you to simmer down," Jenner said coolly. "That money ain't going nowhere. Couple of days from now the posses'll all be gone, then we can go get it. Won't be taking no chances."

Kinkaid brushed his new hat to the back of his head. "Sure, Rufe, there ain't nothing wrong with holding off," he said, eyeing Starbuck slyly. "We won't mind having this jasper around for a spell."

Gorman stared at the Texan briefly, and then a smile spread across his dark features. "Come to think on it, I reckon we might find it real interesting!"

Tinker, unaware of the meaning behind the Texan's words, scrubbed at his jaw. "Just how long you figure we ought to wait, Sid?" he asked.

"Like I said, a couple of days. We're going to be doing a little business with the eastbound stage the day after tomorrow. Be a good time to collect the money."

"For certain," Rufe Gorman said. "Them posses'll have drawed in their tails and lit out for home by then. He won't need to be scared."

Jenner said nothing, simply studied Gorman with his small, mean eyes for a time and then shrugged. Reaching out, he took Starbuck's pistol from its holster and thrust it under his belt.

"Won't be needing that iron," he said, "us all being friends now. Meantime, just make yourself to home. The boys'll show you where to do your sleeping."

The outlaw chief turned away, moved off across the sun-baked pound for the mine-shaft entrance.

"Me and Rufe'll be real pleased to show you around the place," Kinkaid said, still grinning.

Shawn gave the pair a slight nod. "Obliged to you, but no need," he said, and shouldering by Reo and Jubal, followed Jenner.

"Now he sure ain't the friendly type, is he?" Gorman's voice was heavy with sarcasm. "You'd figure him being new and joining up with us and all that, he'd sort of want to know what's what."

"He'll find out, I reckon," Kinkaid replied in lazy fashion. "Could be the hard way, but he'll find out."

Shawn reached the entrance to the shaft, paused, nodded to Monte. The two women with the outlaw, clad in dirt-encrusted, saloon-girl attire, their unkempt hair stringing down about flaccid, painted faces, considered him with interest.

"I'm Myrtha," one said, giggling inanely.

"You going to be around here for a spell?"

"Expect to," Starbuck replied. Voices were coming from inside the mine, and he could see the reflected yellow glow of lamplight.

"What's your name?" the woman continued.

"Calls hisself Starbuck," Monte said thickly, seizing her by the arm. "And you best forget about him unless you're wanting a working over from me!"

"She's all yours," Shawn murmured, and avoiding the second woman, stepped into the shaft.

The corridor he had entered was fairly wide. The light he had noticed was coming from somewhere farther on. Walking slowly, he covered the intervening distance, halted when he came to a turnoff.

What had once been the site of considerable digging had become a fair-sized room. Mattresses lay on the ground against the walls, and in the center was a crude table upon which was a lamp. Benches placed nearby served as chairs.

The corridor continued on to his right, and coming about, he saw the glow of more light and once again caught the sound of voices. Resuming his deliberate pace, he proceeded, noting as he passed two more excavated chambers off the tunnel, both of which were dark but evidently served as sleeping quarters.

He came again to a termination and found himself in the opening to a room much larger than the others. Jenner, sitting at a table, a bottle and several glasses before him, looked up. There were two women with him, one a girl little more than in her midteens and showing considerable less wear than those he'd met outside, the other in the same class and condition as Myrtha and her counterpart. As in the other chambers, a bed consisting only of a mattress on the bare floor served for sleeping purposes.

"See you found your way," the outlaw said. "Guess you're entitled to a drink and a few words on how things are around here. . . . Come in, sit."

Shawn entered the shadowy, cavelike room. It was cool, but the smell of kerosene smoke hung heavy in the air, mixing with a dank staleness. Selecting one of the benches, he sat down at the table, aware of the close scrutiny he was undergoing by the women.

Jenner filled a glass, pushed it at Starbuck, refilled his own. Raising it in salute, he said, *"Salud!"* and downed it.

Shawn drank, set the glass back on the table's rough surface. "Got yourself quite a hotel here," he said. "Be plenty hard for somebody to dig you out."

The outlaw bobbed his head. "Would be at that," he replied. "Nobody's ever tried, however, mainly became nobody's ever found it. Plenty ready if they do. Shaft runs on for a piece, then comes out on the yonder side of the mountain."

Starbuck nodded his approval. "No chance of them ever trapping you, then. . . . About as good a hideout as I've ever come across."

"Can say that for sure." Jenner filled his glass again, made no second offer to Shawn. "Don't know if you've been told, but you'll do your sleeping back up the tunnel in one of the other rooms. Keep this one for myself — and my little friend here. Sort of head-quarters, I reckon you could call it."

"It make any difference if I do my sleeping out in the open?" Shawn asked. "Never did hold with caves and mines and the like."

"You sleep inside like all of us," Jenner said flatly. "Don't want nobody outside, just in case we have to pull out fast — the back way."

"I see. . . ."

"Now, the women. Far as they go they're all spoke for. Amy here," he said putting his arm around the young girl, and jerking her roughly to him, "is my private property. Abby," he added ducking his head at the older woman, "belongs to Reo Pierce. . . . She claims they're going to get hitched."

The woman nodded solemnly. "First chance we get," she stated.

"You would've seen the other two when you come in, Monte's gal Myrtha and Fay. She's Rufe's. . . . Once you get yourself settled in, you can find a woman you want, bring her here. Only thing, once she comes, she don't never leave unless we all do. Want you to make that plain to her."

Shawn nodded his understanding. "Kind of got one picked out already," he said, an idea coming to him. "Girl down at Dooley's. Calls herself Clarissa. Took a shine to her first off."

Jenner was staring into his glass. Abby was picking at a bit of fried food crusted on the front of her dress. Amy, eyes closed, seemed content to just lean against the outlaw.

"Best you do some thinking first about her," he said finally. "She's the kind to give a man trouble. Doubt you could ever bring her to time."

114

"She been here before?"

"Nope, never brought her to the camp. She's a hard one to handle and just ain't worth the hassling it'd take. Mind what I tell you now, and do some tall thinking about her."

"Sure will. . . . Didn't notice where you do your cooking and eating."

"We don't — leastwise not here. Use that old Mex woman down the canyon for that. I buy the grub, and she does all the fixing. That way there ain't no smoke for anybody to see and come looking for."

Shawn again expressed his approval, got to his feet. "I'll say it twice, you've got everything worked out just right. Can see now why you've got the law scratching their heads over you. . . . Guess I'll keep on moseying along, have myself a look around outside."

"Help yourself — only don't go wandering off. Boys ain't too sold on you yet."

Starbuck grinned, turned away. "Got that idea myself," he said. "Obliged to you for the drink."

13

The following morning Starbuck, after a chilly night inside the mine shaft, rode with the outlaws to Maria's and joined them in a breakfast of fried eggs, meat, tortillas, and a thick, black liquid that passed as coffee but that was palatable only after being laced with whiskey.

Two meals per day was the rule, Jenner informed him, although for a few nickels it was possible to visit the Mexican woman's place at any time between regular feedings and satisfy a hunger. In his case, however, it would be necessary that he forego the privilege until everyone was satisfied he could be trusted. Once that point was reached, he could move about pretty much as he pleased.

"Expect I can manage to get by till supper," Shawn said as they mounted and headed back for the hideout.

The women rode double behind their men and partook freely of the bottles of liquor that were being passed between the outlaws.

"Just you make yourself right at home,"

Jenner, in an expansive, genial mood, said. "Do whatever you take the notion to, long as you don't leave the camp. Drinking up's all right long as we ain't planning to do something. The day we've got work to do, then every man jack lays off the bottle and toes the mark."

An argument broke out between Monte and Saul Tinker a mile short of the camp, both men piling off their horses and going at it rough and tumble while the others paused to watch and shout encouragement. It was over quickly, with no one the apparent victor, and after they had remounted, the party continued on.

Reaching the old abandoned mine, Shawn had his first look at the outlaw's stock of horses. Each man looked after his own mount, unless he could persuade another to do the chore for him, and Starbuck, leading the bay Jenner had chosen for him into the makeshift barn, was surprised to see the number of animals in the string.

There were at least two dozen standing about in the structure that had been gutted to accommodate them and in the brush-screened yard behind it. The majority of the stock was unbranded for use during raids, but there were a few bearing owners' marks, all no doubt legally acquired by Sid Jenner and ridden at those times when the outlaws were visiting some town where business of a lawful nature was to be transacted.

He wasn't going to enjoy much freedom in the camp, Shawn realized a time later as he wandered about the old buildings. He needed a few minutes alone in which to write his message to Bill Granett and summon the aid he now must have.

But no matter where he went — the stable, the old miners' shacks, the sunny slopes adjacent to the clearing, one of the outlaws was always loitering nearby. Finally, he gave it up; he would find the necessary minutes during the night to compose the note.

There was little to the camp, and that puzzled him. Sid Jenner and his men had been marauding the area for a considerable length of time and enjoying surprising success in their robbing of banks, stagecoaches, and business houses, yet there was no evidence of such.

What had become of all of the stolen money? The hide-out reflected only the poorest quarters, their weapons, gear, and clothing no better than the poorest working cowhand, their women, ordinarily flashily outfitted by men of such calling, pitiful in their ragged slovenliness. There was more to Sid Jenner than one saw on the surface, Starbuck concluded, one with a deep-seated purpose likely not exhibited to his followers.

It was less difficult to understand the status of the men. Their share of any loot taken — one-sixth each of the half allotted them by their chief — would be small unless the amount taken in the holdup was unusually large. Most of it would be spent quickly on whiskey, gambling, and if in Hackberry or some visited town, other women.

Like trail hands at the end of a drive, money, when they suddenly came into possession of it, flowed from them like water in a mountain stream, and in only a short time they would find themselves flat broke.

Squatting on his haunches against the side of an old shack, Starbuck let his eyes run over the camp. Jenner was inside the shaft, probably in what he termed his headquarters, and in the company of Amy. Reo Pierce was sprawled in the sun not far from the entrance to the mine, a half-empty bottle of whiskey clutched in his hand as he slept.

Elsewhere, Gorman, Kinkaid, and Jubal

were engaged in a game of three-handed poker while two of the women looked on. Monte and Tinker, who seemed to have a greater interest in his movements, were at opposite sides of the small clearing. The scuffle along the trail had not settled the problem between them, and time and again harsh comments passed between them. None of the others seemed to notice, but over all there was an air of sullenness, and quarreling broke out at the slightest provocation.

Shawn glanced to the sky. Midday. The hours were dragging by with painful slowness. Rising, he turned his attention to the mountain in which the shaft had been sunk. Earlier Jenner had mentioned an exit on the opposite side of the formation. He had thought then that he should locate it, get its position fixed in his mind. This would be a good opportunity, assuming Saul Tinker, Monte, or one of the other men did not stop him.

Moving leisurely toward the trail he could see tracing up the slope to the north of the buttelike face of the mountain, he slid a glance at the outlaws.

There was no warning shout, and he continued, reaching the foot of the path and beginning the ascent. It ran directly up for a few paces and then veered left to swing across the slope in a gradually rising tangent.

Starbuck moved on, pausing occasionally to look out upon the country unfurling below. He could see Maria's place, a small, cleared patch on the landscape but so near the general color with its adobe structures and brush fencing as to blend perfectly with the sameness of its surroundings. A narrow, winding strip of silver marked the stream that cut down from higher regions, passing along the fringe of the outlaw camp, hesitating long enough to form a mirrorlike pond at the Mexican woman's *jacal*, then flowing on.

Starbuck continued his climb, circling the brow of the hill and coming finally out into a second canyon running at right angles to the main slash. Two-thirds of the way down the slope, he discovered the exit Sid Jenner had mentioned. It was a fair-sized opening through which a man could crawl with ease.

Taking landmarks, he dropped back onto the weed-overgrown path that led from the exit and followed it. It became apparent shortly that it led back to the camp by a round about route, ending somewhere below the corral in which the horses were held.

The advantage of such was immediately evident; the outlaws, if one day driven into their hiding place in the mountain, had only to leave the mine by the rear opening and circle unseen to where they could reach their horses and make an escape. Sid Jenner had carefully planned to —

Shawn halted. Stepping abruptly from behind a shoulder of rocks were Rufe Gorman, Kinkaid, and Monte. Both Gorman and the Texan wore confident, expectant grins on their swarthy, bewhiskered faces.

"Been wanting to do a little settling up with you, dude," Gorman said.

"Same here," Kinkaid drawled. "Aim to take the price of a new hat out of your hide."

Starbuck folded his arms, leaned against the bulge of granite, and glanced at Monte. "You got something in mind, too?"

The outlaw spat a stream of tobacco juice into the brush, shook his head. "Just come for the show."

"It won't last long," Rufe said, and lunged suddenly.

Starbuck jerked away from the shoulder of rock. The outlaw, endeavoring to check his forward motion, stumbled. Shawn swung a down-sledging right fist backed by everything he had. It caught Gorman on the ear, dropped him to the gravelly pathway like an axed steer.

Starbuck spun, knowing that Kinkaid would be after him in that same moment. He saw the blur of motion as the man rushed in, tried to sidestep. Off balance, he took a hard blow in the ribs as the Texan looped a wild right at him, absorbed another as the outlaw's fist smashed into his shoulder and rocked him to one side.

Sucking for wind, Shawn pivoted away, then halted abruptly and set himself firmly as Kinkaid, grinning broadly, flushed with success, closed in. Starbuck met the rush with a stiff left to the outlaw's nose that brought a gush of blood, crossed with a right that drove him to his heels.

Flicking a glance at Gorman, now pulling himself up to hands and knees, Shawn, moving like a shadow, drove a tattoo of rights and lefts into the dazed Kinkaid's face, wheeled, and raising his leg, booted Gorman solidly in the ribs, sent him rolling off into the brush.

Coming swiftly about, he turned his attention once more to the Texan, flicking him sharply with a left to the face that brought more blood, this time from the mouth, jolted him again with a solid blow to the jaw.

As Kinkaid began to weave on his feet, Starbuck could see Gorman struggling to rise in the welter of loose rock and weeds into which he had plunged and start back for the path. At once Shawn began to move toward the outlaw, prepared to down him for a third time. He heard the rattle of loose gravel behind him, realized that Monte had forsaken his role of spectator, was now cutting himself in on the fight. He turned, took a blow on the shoulder as Monte clubbed him with his pistol.

Anger suddenly roaring through him, Starbuck lashed out at Monte's jaw. His knotted fist connected instead with the side of the man's head. The outlaw howled, staggered back, dropping the weapon he held. Shawn bent hurriedly, scooped up the pistol, and pulled aside. He had an equalizer now, and if they chose to —

Sweat pouring off his features, Starbuck settled gently on his heels. Rufe was on his feet at the edge of the trail, arms hanging loosely at his sides. A few steps away Kinkaid also was standing slack and motionless. Beyond them was Sid Jenner, a pistol in his hand. His small, hard eyes were on Shawn.

"I'll take that gun," he said coldly. "Rest of you, get the hell back to camp."

14

Starbuck shrugged, reversed his grip on Monte's pistol, and tossed it to Jenner. The outlaw leader caught it neatly, passed it on to its owner as the man, trailing the still-dazed Texan and the glowering Rufe Gorman, moved by him on the way to the clearing.

"Plenty handy with your fists," Jenner said, crossing to where Shawn stood.

"Man learns to take care of himself. A gun's not always the answer."

"Seen a bit more there than just taking care of yourself," the outlaw said, holstering his weapon. "Last time I seen something like that was in New York. Man from England calling himself the world's champion fought a match with some jasper who claimed he was the American champion."

"How long ago was that?" Starbuck asked, coming to quick attention.

Jenner's brows lifted, "Oh, been five or six years, I reckon."

Starbuck let it slip from his mind. It could have been Ben in a match with the

Englishman, but it was too far in the past to mean anything.

"Why?"

"Thought it might've been my brother. I'm looking for him, but being that long ago it won't help."

"He a fighter — scientific boxer I think they call themselves?"

Starbuck nodded. "Puts on exhibitions now and then."

"Was quite a show you just put on. Seems you know quite a bit about it, too. What was that fight over?"

Starbuck again brushed at the sweat on his face. "Grudge, nothing more. Shot Kinkaid's hat off his head that day in Junction City and buffaloed Gorman when he got out of line in the saloon."

A slow smile cracked Jenner's lips. "Monte?"

"Said he came along for the show, then decided to take a hand."

"I'd say he made a mistake," the outlaw commented. "Same with Kinkaid and Rufe." He glanced toward the camp. "Like to have a few words with you."

Starbuck studied the man quietly. Sid Jenner was like a chameleon. Around his outlaw followers he seemed on one and the same level; away from them he appeared of better stock and graced with higher education.

"Shoot."

The outlaw, evidently reassured that they were alone, settled on a flat ledge a step off the trail, nodded at Starbuck in friendly fashion.

"I've taken a liking to you," he said. "Something I've made a practice of never doing. Expect it's mostly because you're different from the bunch I'm forced to associate with."

Starbuck leaned back against the shoulder of rock. "Man can pick his own friends if he wants to."

"I don't consider them friends, only tools to work with," Jenner said dryly. "Relief to have somebody like you around. All I can do to stomach that bunch. Got the instincts of a hog, every one of them, wallowing in their own filth, living for nothing more than whiskey and those sluts they call women."

Shawn remained silent but he was thinking ahead, wondering what it was all leading up to.

"I'm about ready to call this dog's life I'm living quits. Only reason I'm here is to get the stake I set out after four years ago to raise, and I've just about made it. . . .

You understand what I'm saying?"

"Sure."

"A few more jobs and the half of that money you'll be turning over to me, and I'll have it."

"Then you figure to quit, go back to New York?"

"Not there — Texas. Going to take the cash I've salted away, go into the saloon and gambling business. Trail town over on the Canadian River. Man can make himself a fortune there if he runs things right. You been over there?"

"Few times."

"Then you know what I mean. I'll be right in the middle of those long drives. Cowhands'll all be rearing to blow every dime they've got."

"Likely won't have any dimes to blow — not at that point of a drive. They don't get paid until they've got the cattle to the place where they're to be sold."

"Realize that, and it's what makes my plan a dead-sure winner. I'll take chits for what they spend if they're short of cash."

Shawn frowned. "Chits? How'll you collect?"

"I'll set it up with the trail boss or the owner of the herd ahead of time, get them to agree to honor the chits up to the amount the drover will get paid. Then I'll have a man waiting for them at the end of the drive, collect from their boss."

"Hardly pay to send a man all that way —"

"Will if he's there to collect from the hands of a half a dozen or more trail herds, and that's what I'm expecting to do. My place'll be where all the drives going to Dodge City, Wichita, and the like will pass right by. Way I see it I'll be doing a land-office business first year."

Starbuck shrugged. It was an ingenious plan, and having made a few trail drives himself and being well acquainted with the minds of men engaged in the hard, trying chore of moving cattle over long distances, there was little doubt but that Sid Jenner would meet with success.

After a time he asked the obvious question. "You telling me about it for some reason?"

Jenner came off the ledge, moved nearer. His ruddy features were intent, and there was a bright gleam in his small eyes.

"Matter of fact I am — a special reason. I'm going to need a good man working for me — several to be exact — but one in particular that I can trust all the way. I'll even be willing to take him in as a partner if he turns out to be what I want."

"And you're thinking I'm that man?"

Jenner nodded. "Been watching you close. You're smart, you've got good common sense, and you can take care of yourself. Seeing you handle Rufe and those other two made up my mind for me."

"Not sure I —"

"Hold on a minute before you say anything. Let me give you the whole ball of wax. That seventy-five hundred you've got cached, half's mine, the rest's supposed to be divided among all of you. What if we keep it all for ourselves?"

Shawn feigned surprise — and interest. "Be a little hard to mange."

"Not if I arrange it. Can say that tomorrow when you went to get it, it was gone. Somebody found it and took off. There's no way any of the bunch could prove you were lying, and if I say that I believe you, that'll end it."

"We'd split fifty-fifty, that it?"

"More or less. You'd take your half and turn it over to me, too, buy yourself into my deal."

"Be a partner right off?"

Jenner rubbed at his jaw. "Well, half of seventy-five hundred won't buy you a full partnership, but it'd be a start. You'd increase your share by working. . . . I figure you'd be a top choice for doing the col-

130

lecting at the end of the drives."

Starbuck gave the offer apparent thought. There was little else to do but indicate interest and play along with the outlaw chief. Letting Jenner believe that he would throw in with him in his scheme could make matters easier insofar as the remaining members of the gang were concerned. He would need greater freedom to move about in the next few days if he was to get word to the U.S. marshal in Santa Fe and be ready for the federal lawman's posse when it arrived.

"Not sure I savvy how it'd work," he said. "If I was to go in with you, I'd like to know how fast I could build my part up to where I'd be half owner."

"Be up to you. I'd be willing to pay you plenty for taking on the job of settling up with the drovers. The more of what you earn that you'd put back into the business, the sooner you'd be a full partner. . . . I'd say a couple of years if you didn't mind living cheap."

"No problem there," Shawn said, looking thoughtfully into the distance. "Sort of used to that. Mind if I do some studying on it?"

Jenner smiled. "Hell, no! Would've been disappointed in you if you hadn't wanted to. One reason took to you right off —

you're no gut-hungry, whiskey-loving, woman chaser looking for a quick dollar like the others — you've got to think everything right through to the finish.

"But you'd best have your mind made up by morning. We'll have to pull that stunt about somebody finding the money when we ride in to tap that stage."

"Give you my answer before we head out," Starbuck promised.

15

"I'm taking your offer," Starbuck said to Sid Jenner that next morning as they rode down to Maria's for the early meal.

The outlaw chief glanced about at the other members of the party, shook his head indicating that it was neither the time nor the place to discuss the matter.

"Later," he murmured.

They ate their breakfast, made the return trip to camp without any more passing between them, but near noon, as preparations were under way for the stagecoach holdup, Jenner crossed the clearing to where Shawn was saddling the horse he was to ride that day. Several of the men had already finished the chore and were standing idly by watching those yet to complete the task.

"You'll be needing this," Jenner said, and handed Starbuck his pistol.

Reo Pierce paused, threw a glance at his fellow outlaws. "Now, that ain't smart, Sid!" he said protestingly.

"Whoever's got his rifle, give it back,"

Jenner continued, and then turned to face Pierce. "When did you start deciding what was what around here?"

The eyes of the two men locked, held briefly until Pierce looked away. "Only meaning that we don't know nothing for sure about him yet."

"I do, and that's what counts in this outfit," Jenner said coldly. "Seems you forgot that. Starbuck's one of us. He's going on the raid, and while we're doing that, he'll dig up that money he buried and meet us back here at camp with it."

"If he don't keep on going with it," Rufe Gorman said sourly. His jaw was badly swollen, and the lump above his temple was still prominent.

"You'd be dumb enough to try that if it was you," Jenner said icily. "But he ain't you, luckily. Knows damn well if he takes one step out of this valley, he's dead. I know it, same as he does, and if it hasn't sunk through your thick skull yet, then there ain't much hope."

Gorman stirred sullenly, turned back to his horse. Jenner, point made, wheeled, retraced his steps to the mine-shaft entrance. Saul Tinker moved up to Shawn, handed him the rifle.

"Reckon this is yours."

Starbuck nodded, slid the weapon into the saddle boot. "Belongs to that deputy," he said, grinning. "I sort of took it."

The outlaw smiled appreciatively, began to draw on a long, faded dust coat. Others in the gang were doing likewise. Starbuck glanced around.

"There an extra one of those?"

Tinker said, "Nope, man has to buy his own. You got a slicker?"

"Yeh — back on my saddle in Junction City."

Saul ducked into the stable, reappeared shortly with an oilskin coat, tossed it to Shawn.

"Can use mine this time. Best you stop by that saddle shop in town, get yourself fixed up proper."

"Obliged, I'll do that," Starbuck said, drawing on the stiff yellow rainwear.

Making a final check of his gear, he swung onto his horse and settled himself. Most of the others had mounted, were waiting for Sid Jenner to appear. The outlaw leader, as if waiting until everybody was ready, came from the mine-shaft entrance in that next moment, strode briskly across the hardpack, and stepped up onto his saddle. Without speaking, he cut his mount about and struck off down the slope in the general direction of Hackberry.

They rode in a loosely knit group, Jenner near center and slightly ahead. Reo Pierce was to his left, the glum Rufe Gorman on his right. Kinkaid, also showing the effects of the previous day's encounter, was maintaining a morose silence along with the remaining outlaws.

Starbuck, fully aware of the atmosphere of hostility, kept his horse to the edge of the party. His position among the men was becoming increasingly precarious, particularly so now that Sid Jenner had declared himself. He'd be lucky, he reckoned, if he was able to complete his plan and get free of the outlaw band without taking a bullet in the back.

But the end was in sight. During the night while the others slept, he had written the note to Bill Granett giving instructions as to where and when to meet him with a posse. He would halt the stage and pass the letter to the driver with instructions to have the message telegraphed to the lawman at the first town where such facilities were available. Once that was done, he had but to walk the narrow line of care until the hour of the meeting with Granett and his armed men, and then he could bring it all to a close.

They reached the road that led to the settlement, pulled to a stop. Jenner swung about, faced his followers.

"Stage is due in less'n an hour. We'll hit it in that canyon above five miles the other side of town this time."

He paused, looked over the party as if expecting question or comment. There was neither.

"Starbuck," he continued, "want you to head on up to where you hid that money. Dig it up and get on back to camp. We'll meet you there after we've cleaned out that stage."

"Ain't you sending somebody with him?" Pierce demanded, suddenly finding his voice.

"No need," Jenner said quietly. "He knows what's good for him — and I been over that once. Anyway, he tries running, I'll track him down and get him — if the law don't beat me to it. You got that straight, Starbuck?"

Shawn nodded. "I'll be waiting at camp. Not a fool."

Reo Pierce swore gustily. "Still think you're loco to let him go alone."

Sid Jenner, hands resting on the horn of his saddle, gave it consideration. Tension began to stir through Starbuck. Having one of the outlaws riding with him, looking over his shoulder and regarding his every move with suspicion, would create insurmountable problems, make it impossible to get the note to Granett into the coach driver's hands.

"I don't," the outlaw chief said patiently. "Besides, I'll be needing every one of you. Big payroll on that stage. Can expect a guard inside as well as the one riding shotgun. Could even be more. . . . Move out, Starbuck."

Shawn sighed inwardly in relief as he cut his horse about and spurred off up the road; Jenner was taking no chance on his being interfered with.

Minutes later, he glanced over his shoulder. The outlaws were loping slowly toward Hackberry. He made a quick count; seven riders. No one had dropped out to follow and keep him under observation — yet. But that was not saying there wouldn't be. Any one of the men could take it on himself to slip off, double back — and as far as Sid Jenner was concerned, he trusted him just about as far as he knew the outlaw in turn trusted him.

He rode on, keeping in the open and in full view until he made the first bend in the road. At once he roweled his horse to a gallop, and angled directly into the brush and trees lying to his right. When he was a distance up on the slope, he drew to a halt and, hidden behind a dense clump of cedars, waited.

A quarter hour passed, a half. No rider appeared on the road. He dared wait no longer since the stage holdup would soon be taking place, and he must have what he had in mind completed well before the outlaws were finished.

Jenner was trusting him, it seemed, but then he hardly had a choice; he couldn't afford to allow one of his men to witness the recovering of the cash box. It was to be reported stolen, dug up by someone who disappeared with it. At least, that was the way it was set up to be between him and Sid Jenner, but it was always better to assume nothing as certain when dealing with a man like him.

Cutting back down the slope, he pointed for the finger of rock where he had cached the bank money. Locating the spot with no difficulty, he once more made sure he was not being watched and then dug up the metal container.

Going back onto the saddle, he moved on down the road a distance to where the brush grew thick along its shoulder, and there, after wrapping the packs of currency and the small bags of gold coin in an old undershirt he found in his saddlebags, he buried the money for a second time.

Marking the place well in his mind, he tucked the empty cash box under his arm and, mounting, returned to the road. Proceeding along its dusty width for a mile or so, Starbuck halted finally behind a weedy bulge of earth and settled down to await the stagecoach.

He was in for some tight moments, he realized, and the odds on convincing the outlaws, and now Sid Jenner, that someone had beat him to the money were poor. But it was the only course he could follow; simply taking the box of bank cash and heading for Junction City or one of the other neighboring towns in the hope of getting a lawman to listen and help was not only foolish but dangerous.

Too, such would put Jenner and his crowd, burning with vengeance, on his trail. Unknown to outsiders as they were, they would be able to get to him with no difficulty even if he was fortunate enough to obtain help from a sheriff or marshal.

Flight was something he could not consider, anyway, not if he wished to complete the job of putting an end to the outlaw gang's activities. To leave could also arouse doubts in Sid Jenner's mind, strengthen the belief of Reo Pierce, Gorman, and the others that he was not who he claimed to be, was, in fact, a lawman worming his way into their midst. Jenner, cautious as he was, would take no chances, and the hideout in the mine shaft would be abandoned immediately — certainly long before a posse could be organized and brought in to apprehend the outlaws.

No, he was doing the only thing he could, and success as well as survival depended on his ability to convince Jenner and his gun hands that he was one of them, that the money they were expecting to divide had actually been taken.

Time crawled by slowly. Shawn, off his horse, lounged in the shade of a thick, twisted juniper, ears straining to hear the approach of the stagecoach. It should require only moments to step into the open, flag down the vehicle, pass the note with necessary instructions to the driver. He had a half eagle ready to pay the cost of the telegram, along with the advice to the man to pocket the difference for his trouble. After that he could mount and ride hard for the outlaw camp. The possibility of reaching there ahead of the others should be good.

Forking over five dollars was cutting deep into the last of his cash reserve. He knew it was far more than was necessary, but he wanted to be certain the driver would not fail him, and paying him generously for the favor would ensure completion. He could, of course, have borrowed from the bank's money, leaving with it a note to that effect and replacing it later would have been perfectly agreeable with Charley Grimshaw, the banker, but it had not occurred to Starbuck. If it had, however, he likely would not have availed himself of the privilege. He had been given no permission to do so; therefore, it was unthinkable.

He drew to attention quickly as the distant rattle of the oncoming stage reached him. Immediately, he moved toward the road, threw his glance in the direction of the sound. He swore softly.

The coach was in sight, but on beyond the swaying vehicle and its racing horses, skirting the fringe of brush to its east were two riders. Shawn squinted into the glare striving to make out their identities. . . . Gorman and Kinkaid. Apparently suspicious, they had left the outlaw party on some pretext, were coming to check on him.

He would have to forget passing the message for U.S. Marshal Granett to the driver. Rufe and the Texan would see him halt the stagecoach, instantly become aware that something was wrong.

Wheeling, he dropped back to his horse, mounted, and struck off through the heavy undergrowth for the camp. He would have to make another try to get word out — possibly that next day when the southbound stage would pass. . . . All he needed was an excuse to again be somewhere along the road at the right time.

16

They were waiting for him when he rode in — all but Kinkaid and Gorman — lined up in front of the entrance to the mine. Evidently something had gone wrong, for all appeared to be downcast and in an ugly mood. It occurred instantly to Starbuck that his own salvation lay in a like mien.

Riding up to where the outlaws stood, he threw the empty cash box violently at Sid Jenner's feet.

"Somebody else got there first!" he snarled.

Reo Pierce swore loudly in disgust. Mutterings came from the others. Jenner's stolid expression did not alter, but when his eyes met Starbuck's, he winked slightly.

"Sure as hell not our day," he said wearily. "That payroll wasn't on the stage, either."

Shawn swung off his horse, which immediately turned and moved off toward the stable. Pierce's voice lashed out at him.

"You saying that money was gone?"

"There's the box it was in," Starbuck snapped, his tone equally hard.

The outlaw stared at him for a long moment, spat. "Mighty goddam funny, I'd say."

Playing out the situation to its fullest, Shawn took a long step forward, caught Reo Pierce by the shirt front, jerked him half around.

"You calling me a liar?"

Pierce swore, knocked Starbuck's hand aside, reached for his pistol. He froze, mouth agape, as he looked into the muzzle of Shawn's weapon.

"Want an answer," Starbuck pressed softly.

"Be enough of that!" Jenner's voice broke the sudden hush that had dropped over the clearing. "Both of you — back off."

Pierce, muttering unintelligibly, anger tearing at his dark features, wheeled, stalked off toward the mine's entrance. In the fading tension Starbuck watched him halt and, arms folded, lean sulkily against the rock face of the cliff. Only then did he holster his pistol.

Jenner was studying him narrowly. "You find any signs of who done it?"

"Few tracks. Aim to go back tomorrow and do some trailing."

"Why didn't you do that while you was

there?" Monte demanded. "What'd you want to wait for?"

"Was getting late," Shawn said coolly. "Figured if I didn't show up here soon you'd think I'd hightailed it and the whole bunch of you'd be out gunning for me." He paused, glanced around. "Don't see Gorman or Kinkaid. You send them after me?"

"Stayed in town," Saul Tinker answered before Jenner could reply. "Was mighty put out over that payroll not being on the stage. They was both counting plenty on the money they was to get — same as the rest of us. Now, you coming along saying there won't be no bank money to split —"

"Getting plenty low myself," Starbuck said. "What's the deal on that payroll? Understood the stage would be hauling it."

"So'd we," Monte said, shoulders lifting and falling resignedly.

"Word I get's usually pretty right," Jenner said. "Something must've happened down the line, or I was lied to. Intend to find out which."

"Well, all I can say is it's been a hell of a day," Jubal said as he turned toward the mine shaft. "Ain't nothing gone right."

Saul Tinker and Monte nodded their morose agreement and moved off after

146

him. Tinker said, "Could sure use a drink — I'm plumb out and was aiming to buy me up a supply when we got some cash. . . . How you fixed, Jube?"

Jubal's shoulders twitched. "Got maybe a pint left. Aim to keep it for myself. Anyways, I recollect you owing me from the last time you was busted."

"By hell, I do! Plain slipped my mind — but I'll even up with you this time, first money I get."

Jubal halted at the mouth of the shaft. Abby and Myrtha, smiling, sidled up to him. He glanced at both, turned to Monte and Saul Tinker.

"Expect you'd best rustle up your liquor somewheres else," he sad. "Going to be needing mine."

"Now, Jube —" Tinker protested, following the man and the two women into the shaft. "You and me's been friends for a mighty long time!"

"Same here," Monte added, crowding close behind Saul. "Always been share and share alike with us —"

Starbuck came about, the remainder of the conversation lost. Jenner had not moved, was looking moodily off into the hills. Beyond him Amy had emerged from the mine, was walking toward him.

Continuing, Shawn crossed the hardpack to where his horse waited patiently to be admitted into the stable. The men had accepted his story of the money's loss, now would come the task of convincing Sid Jenner. He readied the sorrel, began to release the saddle cinch. The faint crunch of gravel underfoot told him that the outlaw chief had come up behind him.

"Where'd you hide it?"

Suddenly taut, Starbuck said, "Never brought it. What I told you and the others was straight."

Jenner was silent for a long moment. Then, "You wanting me to believe that money really was gone?"

"Believe what you like. You saw the empty box."

The outlaw cursed deeply. "Thought you was going through all that for the sake of the others." Again he was quiet, moved finally to where he could see Starbuck's face.

"You ain't tricking me, are you — aiming to maybe keep all that cash for yourself? If you are, by God —"

Starbuck shrugged, pulled the saddle from his horse, and straddled it on a nearby rail. "Not that big a fool. Partnership in that gambling house of yours'd be worth a lot more'n seventy-five hundred dollars."

"Could be you changed your mind about that, figured to go it alone. That's a lot of cash."

"Not much use to me dead — which is what I figure I'd be if I tried pulling out — either by your gun or some trigger-happy lawman."

Again Jenner was silent. Loud voices were coming from the mine shaft where the contention between Jubal, Saul Tinker, and Monte had apparently graduated into a full-fledged quarrel.

"Like somebody said, it's been a lousy day," the outlaw leader murmured. "Nothing's gone right. . . . You think there's a chance you can track down whoever it was that took it?"

Starbuck, pulling the bridle off the horse, opened the door, let the animal enter. "Am pretty good at such," he said, adding the headstall to the saddle. "Once did some scouting for the army, learned plenty. Sure aim to try, come tomorrow."

Jenner glanced at the sun. "Yeh, too late now to start. Be dark time you got there. You do much looking around before you headed back?"

The tension within Starbuck was easing off, but slowly. Jenner seemed to be buying his story, was agreeable to his making the trip back to where the money had been buried and starting a search for the thief.

"Some. Found where a horse had been standing and where he was ridden off into the rocks. Going to take some hard work. Country's plenty rough — all shale and gravel."

"Could be for nothing," Jenner said, eyes now on Amy, waiting in the center of the yard where he had halted her. "Whoever it was probably lit out fast when he got his paws on all that money. Look that way to you?"

Shawn leaned against the wall of the stable, brushed at the sweat on his face. The heat was not particularly intense, but the pressure of the minutes laid heavily upon him. If he could be sure the outlaw chief believed him, he could rest easier; earlier, he had felt that he had, but now, with Jenner continuing to question him, he was beginning to wonder.

Damn Gorman and Kinkaid, anyway! If they hadn't shown up, his call for help to Bill Granett in Santa Fe would likely have reached its destination and preparations to act been underway. As it was, he was far from being off the tightrope he had been walking ever since that moment when he'd dumped Deputy Sheriff Egan from the buckboard and taken charge of the bank's money.

"Not sure it was an outsider," he said, striving to put the matter on a more solid footing. "Got a hunch it was somebody in town — Hackberry."

Sid Jenner frowned. "What's set you to thinking that?"

"Was nobody else on the road the day I cached the box. Nobody except you and the rest of the outfit — and me."

"Guess that's right —"

"And I didn't see anybody riding through after I got to town. Would've spotted them. It's set me to wondering if one of the storekeepers or some of the hired help was out there, maybe taking a drive or delivering something to a customer —"

"And seen you burying that box," the outlaw completed. "Then when you'd gone, and we'd pulled out, he dug it up. . . . By God, Starbuck, you maybe've got something there! It could mighty easy be one of them penny-pinching counter jumpers!"

"Just a hunch —"

"But a plenty good one, and more I

think on it, the more sense it makes. Why, goddam them, we've never touched a hair in that town! Left them alone, even kept others out so's they wouldn't be bothered, and all I asked for was for them to not do any talking about us to the law or anybody else that come along asking questions. . . . That's all I ever wanted from them!"

"There's nothing for sure," Shawn said, trying to stem the man's rising anger. "First let me —"

"If I've been crossed," Jenner raged in a trembling voice, "by God I'll take that dump apart board by board, burn it to the ground!"

Starbuck caught the outlaw by the arm. "Hold on, now! You're moving too fast. First off, me thinking it maybe was somebody from the town's only a hunch. Nothing for sure, but if it was, you've got to remember that folks there didn't know you had any claim on the money. They figures it was me they were skinning."

Pierce and the woman, Fay, apparently attracted by Jenner's raised voice, had come from the mine shaft, were now standing before the opening. The woman said something to Amy who only shook her head.

Sid Jenner looked down, rubbed his jaw

nervously. "Reckon you're right," he said, temper cooling. "Whoever done it didn't know, but that don't mean I won't do what I have to, to get it back. I'll put it up to Dooley and them others, tell them they'll find out who it was and make him fork it over or I'll —"

"Give me the chance to do some tracking first," Starbuck broke in. "Could be I'm wrong, and you sure don't want to make a fool of yourself. . . . If that trail leads to town, then you can start cracking your whip."

The outlaw, calm now, nodded in agreement. "Just what we'll do, but I'm betting you've got it figured right."

"We'll know tomorrow, once I get to work."

"When'll you be going?"

"In the morning — late. Sign shows up better when the sun's high."

Sid Jenner looked puzzled for a moment, shrugged. "Well, you're the one doing it," he said, and shifted his glance to the slope.

Rufe Gorman and Kinkaid were just breaking out of the brush that masked the trail. Both men appeared worn and dusty, and there was anger in their eyes.

"You go on about your business," Jenner said quietly. "Best you leave Rufe and

Amos to me. Don't want you mixing it up with them like you did with Reo."

"As soon have it out now —"

"Expect you would, but it ain't what I want. Don't want nothing happening to you — and you taking on the both of them, it could. Whatever they got crossways in their craw, I'll straighten out."

Starbuck continued to hesitate, and then concluding it was wise to obey the outlaw chief if for no other reason than to remain in his good graces, he wheeled and went into the stable.

17

He had suspected that Sid Jenner would not permit his going back to the valley alone to begin the search for the alleged theft of the bank's money; such would have been good luck far beyond belief. But he had not expected the entire gang to accompany him. He made no comment on it, however, when that next morning, he found the others, surly and uncommunicative, also saddling their mounts for the ride in.

When all were ready and Jubal had led the outlaw leader's mount into the open, Jenner came from the shaft and swung onto the saddle.

"Figured you could use all the help you could get," he said, his small, hard eyes considering Starbuck with unblinking candor.

Shawn stirred indifferently while doubts that Jenner had not believed his story again rose within him.

"Be better if I worked alone. All these horses walking about could mess up the tracks."

"Boys'll be careful," the outlaw said, and roweling his mount, headed for the trail.

They halted at Maria's for a quick breakfast, then rode on, reaching the Hackberry road around midmorning. Coming to a stop there, Jenner turned to Shawn.

"Your party now," he said. "Lead the way."

Starbuck cut his horse around and loped the distance to the finger of rock where he had originally buried the cash box. Drawing up by a squat cedar, he dismounted, pointed to the hole in the ground.

"That's where it was," he said, and still hoping to rid himself of the outlaw party — or most of it — added, "aim to start here looking for tracks. Be obliged to you all if you'll stay clear."

"Reckon you ain't the only tracker in the country," Reo Pierce said, and came off his horse.

Starbuck shrugged. The possibility of getting the message he had written to Granett in Santa Fe was becoming more remote with each passing minute. With so many outlaws around, he would never be able to hand the note to the driver of the stage when it arrived. An idea came to him, one that just might help.

Folding his arms in apparent resignation, he cocked his head at Jenner, said, "I thought we had a deal."

The outlaw leader stiffened at the loaded comment. He frowned, glanced about at his followers, who had turned, were facing him questioningly.

"Starbuck's talking about this tracking he figures to do," he said with a forced grin. "Told him I'd give him a free hand at it."

Shawn suppressed a smile. Sid Jenner would not thank him for that remark, but it could have the desired result.

"Won't get much done — not with this whole bunch tramping around here."

"Well, I ain't leaving," Pierce declared stubbornly. "Aiming to sick right with you."

Jenner gave it all consideration, put his attention back on Shawn. "It be all right if Reo stays?"

He wanted no one at all, of course, but it would be unwise to protest further. To do so could only arouse suspicion. He'd manage to shake Pierce somehow.

"All right," he said. "But he'll be doing what I tell him. Can't waste time walking on each other's heels."

Reo Pierce grumbled a reply. Jenner

nodded, said, "There something the rest of us can be doing?"

"Get to town," Starbuck said promptly. "Keep your eye on things — you know what I mean. If there's a stranger hanging around waiting for the stage, keep tabs on him. Could be the man we're looking for."

"Just what we'll do —"

"Same goes for any of the folks living there regular. If they take a notion to catch the stage, be a good idea to stop them. What time does it go through today?"

"Around noon, heading south."

"Good enough," Starbuck said. He knew now when to expect the stagecoach. "We have some luck, we'll join you in town later."

Sid Jenner raised his hand, waved his riders toward the road. Reaching there, he pulled to a stop, allowed the others to continue on. Twisting about on his saddle, he beckoned to Shawn.

"You trying to get me shot?" he asked in a low voice as Starbuck drew close. "You had the boys thinking —"

"Trying to get them out of my hair so's I can run down that money," Starbuck countered. "We can forget keeping it all if one of them's around when I find it."

Jenner studied him with his cold, dark

eyes. After a moment he made a slight gesture toward Pierce. "What about Reo?"

"Makes it tough, but I'll try shaking him."

"Well, if you come across the money, and he's in the way, use that gun you're carrying. What it's for," the outlaw said, and spurring his horse, hurried to catch up with his men.

Shawn turned back to where Pierce was waiting, an angry, suspicious set to his features.

"What was that all about?"

"Little private business between Sid and me," Starbuck replied indifferently. "Something we'll be taking care of later at Dooley's."

Reo Pierce's color deepened. That he was smarting under the belief that his position as second in command of the gang and the acknowledged right hand of Jenner had been usurped was apparent.

"He never said nothing to me about you and him having some business. And that there deal, you was saying something —"

"You want to complain, go see Jenner," Shawn broke in, cutting short the peevish protesting, and moved on to the small excavation where the box had been buried.

Making a pretense of examining the area

carefully, Shawn began to range wider, eyes on the hard, flinty soil. Pierce had not stirred but remained at the side of his horse seemingly caught up by indecision and suspicion.

Abruptly, Starbuck wheeled, returned to the bay, and stepped into the saddle.

"You find something?" Reo asked, coming to life.

"Been a horse take out across that hump," he said, pointing to a roll of land a short distance away. "Could be what I'm looking for."

Pierce nodded, mounted his animal. Shawn said, "Be a waste of time for us both to follow the tracks. Smarter if one of us would drop back to the road, circle, and try to pick up the trail on the yonder side of this mountain."

"Yeh, reckon it would," the outlaw said, his eyes narrowing.

"Can do that myself. You start from here. I spot the tracks, I'll signal."

"Nope," Pierce said flatly, "you do the starting here. I'll go around to the other side."

Shawn's shoulders stirred as he masked a smile. It had worked perfectly. Now, with the outlaw out of the way, he would be able to halt the stage with no interference.

But, suspicious as the outlaw was, he'd best make a show of disappointment.

"Still think I ought to do the circling, but I won't argue with you. Besides, trail's getting colder, and if the wind gets up, we'll sure lose it."

Pierce said nothing, simply spurred his horse about and moved toward the road.

"You spot the tracks — big horse with one worn shoe — fire a shot, and I'll come fast."

The outlaw nodded and continued on his way.

Shawn urged the bay forward, began to ascend the slope. He glanced at the sun. Still an hour or more before he could expect the stagecoach to pass. He would start working the rise, giving the appearance of following a trail in the event Reo Pierce decided to double back and do some checking before he got too far down the road.

Then, when he was certain there was no longer any danger from the outlaw, he would return, angle across the hills, and intercept the coach a safe distance from the area.

A half hour later, after seeing no sign of Reo Pierce, Shawn swung around and rode a good two miles north and there dropped down to the road. Choosing a good point where a bend would shut off the view of anyone coming up from the direction of Hackberry, he dismounted and made himself comfortable in the shade of a small tree.

The stage was not long in arriving, and again taking a swift canvass of the surrounding country to be certain Pierce or no one else was in the area, he took up a position in the center of the highway. The coach, with only a driver on the box and two women passengers inside, came to a quick halt at sight of him.

"Ain't carrying nothing but a couple'a ladies," the driver said, his face angry. He was an elderly man with a square-cut, tobacco-stained beard and colorless eyes. "Plumb wasted your time, friend."

Starbuck climbed up onto the seat beside him, ignoring the sounds of fright coming from the interior of the vehicle.

"Not holding you up," he said, reaching inside his shirt and producing the note he'd prepared. "Like for you to get this to the first telegraph office you come to."

The driver frowned, looked at the folded sheet of paper. "That'll be Jonesboro. Due there late this afternoon — it's the reg'lar night stop."

"Be fine," Starbuck said, handing him the half eagle he'd set aside for the purpose. "Important thing is to get it sent. Appreciate it if you'll stand right there till you're sure the telegraph operator's got it on the way. . . . Don't know what it'll cost, but this ought to more than cover it. What's left is yours for your trouble."

The old man bobbed his head, thrust the note and the gold coin into his shirt pocket. "It'll be like you're wanting. I'll have 'er fired off quick as I get to 'Boro — and I'll stay there till he's done. It something real important?"

"Plenty," Shawn said, dropping back to the ground. "I'll take it as a favor if you don't do any talking about it."

"Sure enough," the driver said, and slapping the lines, sent his team lunging into forward motion again.

Satisfaction running through him, Starbuck returned to the bay and, vaulting onto the saddle, headed back up the hillside. He had word on the way now to the U.S. marshal; the help he needed could be expected to arrive by dark that next day. . . . All that was necessary now was for him to keep the outlaws believing in him until that hour came.

18

Starbuck spent the better part of two hours working the hillside, painstakingly from all appearances, ferreting out the tracks of a horse and rider who supposedly had crossed the mountain in that vicinity.

Reaching the opposite side, he saw Reo Pierce near the foot of the grade, off his horse and resting in the thick shade of a small cottonwood. As he rode in close, the outlaw, face shining with sweat, regarded him sourly.

"You find anything?"

"Not sure. Followed some tracks for quite a ways, then lost them in the rocks. Could be the man I'm looking for. You have any luck?"

"Naw," Pierce replied, pulling himself upright. "You aim to keep on?"

Shawn nodded. "With that much money at stake, I'm not about to quit."

"Lot of work for nothing," Pierce grumbled. "That money's long gone. Can kiss it good-bye."

"Not about to — not yet."

"Up to you. Me, I'm heading for town.

You want me saying anything to Sid?"

It was welcome news even though it did come late. Too, it would appear that Reo Pierce had finally accepted him and his story.

"Tell him there's no use waiting if I don't show up by dark. I'll ride straight for camp."

Pierce considered that in his dull, sullen way. Evidently satisfied, he crossed to his horse and mounted. Saying nothing, he rode off the short hill and down the incline to the road. There he halted and, one hand resting on the cantle, turned and faced Starbuck.

"Still ain't sold on you," he called. "Nobody else is, either. Would be plenty smart was you to be bringing that money in when you show up."

"If I find it, I'll do that," Shawn said. "It's how it'd be."

"Best you make a special try — and don't go thinking you can ride out of the country with it. We ain't dumb enough to let you do that."

"I'll see you at camp, come dark, with or without it," Starbuck said evenly. "Depends on how the cards fall."

Pierce digested that slowly and then, clucking to his horse, set off for Hackberry at an easy lope. He was rid of him for the rest of the day, Shawn thought with a sigh, and added to that the hope that none of the other members of the outlaw band would take it on themselves to ride back and insist on giving him a hand in the search.

Moving down into the shadow of the tree vacated by Reo, he dismounted and, finding a flat place, settled himself as comfortably as possible, eyes on the gradually diminishing figures of the outlaw and his horse.

Time would be hanging heavily — and precariously — on his hands, he realized. The best he could hope for was that Bill Granett and his posse would reach the appointed rendezvous by five or six o'clock that next afternoon — almost thirty hours away. That meant he had not only the remainder of that day and night to face but the next as well.

He needed to come up with an idea that would keep Sid Jenner and his gun hands appeased until it was time to slip off and meet the federal lawman and his party — which would be no small accomplishment in itself. But what? Shawn mulled the problem about in his mind, struggling to come up with an idea. He could, he supposed, produce the missing money. It could then be recovered later when he led in the posse and the outlaws were captured.

Such would certainly allay any suspicion the men entertained, but on the other hand, if something went wrong, it could mean the complete loss of the seventy-five hundred dollars in cash — cash for which he felt responsible. After a few minutes' consideration, he decided it was too great a risk and discarded the idea.

Reo Pierce was at last lost to sight. It would be better that he not still be where the outlaw had last seen him should one of the others put in an appearance. Climbing back onto the bay, Starbuck swung on down the slope, gained the road. Careful at such times and always reluctant to take anything for granted, he walked the horse slowly, eyes on the ground as if searching, to the opposite side of the valley until he was well into the brush.

Once in the cover, he veered south, pointing for a ledge of rock he had noted earlier. It was a steep climb, and when he eventually reached it, the gelding was blowing hard for wind, but it was as far as Starbuck intended to go.

Dismounting, he picketed the bay in the deep shade beneath a tight grove of pines and dropped back to the ledge. Working around to its western side from which he had a broad view of the valley and the road to Hackberry, he found a grassy pocket among the rocks and sat down.

Due to the uncertain temper of the out-laws that previous night, he had felt it only prudent to be on guard, thus had slept only fitfully. That, combined with the warmness of the day, at once had its effect on him, and he began to doze. But he need have no fears now, and tipping his hat over his eyes, long legs stretched out before him, head and shoulders against a cool slab of granite, he fell sound asleep.

He awoke to the dry rustling of leaves. Motionless, he opened his eyes slightly. A white-vested gopher was standing upright only an arm's length from him, observing him with bright curiosity. Shawn stirred. In the merest fragment of an instant the ro-dent vanished into the rocks.

Starbuck looked to the sky, cloudless, steel-blue. The sun was low. Four o'clock, perhaps a bit later, he reckoned. He had slept almost the entire afternoon. . . . The arrival time of Marshal Granett and his posse had been cut to twenty-four hours, more or less.

He shifted his attention to the road, let his eyes travel its course from where it be-came visible to him in the north to where it was lost in the short hills to the south. It was deserted. He glanced to the long slopes on the opposite side of the valley, saw no sign of riders. Evidently, no one had returned to take Reo Pierce's place.

He should be heading back to camp. It would be well after dark now before he reached it, but that did not disturb him particularly; the outlaws had finally decided to trust him, it would appear, and every minute ho could manage to be apart from Sid Jenner and his guns lessened the possibility of final plans going awry — as well as the pitch of danger to himself.

It would be a help if he could avoid returning to the camp at all, simply lie low until the posse came; but again the likelihood that such might alarm Jenner and cause him to move hastily and thus escape capture ruled it out.

He could only pursue the plans he had laid, treading carefully, watching his tongue and his actions closely — and hope he could hold it all together until reinforcements came.

Retracing his steps to the bay, he went to the saddle and cut back across to the road. Once on its dusty course, he followed the twin ruts to where he could turn off and point inland for the outlaw hideout.

It was not yet dark when he reached Maria's, and waving the required salutation to her, he continued on his way. The men would have already had their meal, if after a day in Hackberry they bothered to eat at all. Personally, he was feeling the need for food, but it would have to wait; best he put in an appearance at the camp, allay any suspicions or fears that he had deserted, and then visit the Mexican woman's shack.

He gained the first clearing with its scatter of old shacks, angled toward the corner where the trail led into the brush before dropping down to the camp. A rattle of gravel coming from somewhere on the grade behind him caught his attention. . . . Someone else headed for the hideout — only moments behind him.

It could be one of the outlaws — or it could be someone from the town, possibly even an outsider that Jenner depended on for information. It was something he should know. Instantly, Starbuck veered to his left, spurred the bay into the shadows lying back of an old shed.

Shortly, a rider appeared, a hunched shape on a small, gray horse. Shawn stared at the man intently. There was something familiar about him, but in the poor light it was difficult to distinguish characteristics. . . . Elderly, ordinary work clothes, small, sharp face with a square-cut beard.

Starbuck stiffened. It was the stagecoach driver, the one to whom he'd given the message for U.S. Marshal Granett.

19

Grim, Starbuck waited until the man had disappeared into the brush along the base of the cliff, and then, on foot, spurs silenced, he followed. Before he had reached the edge of the lower clearing, he heard the voice of Rufe Gorman sing out.

"Hey, Sid — it's Sam Booker!"

Crouched low, Shawn worked his way through the undergrowth to a point as near the mine's entrance as he dared. All of the outlaws, with the exception of Jenner, were grouped around the opening where some sort of meeting, unattended by their chief, apparently had been under way. The arrival of the driver had interrupted proceedings.

Jenner stepped into the yard. His face was hard-edged, and there was an air of irritability about him, of anger, brought on undoubtedly by the day's failures.

"What's on your mind, Sam?" he barked, taking up a stand in front of the shaft's entrance.

The driver dug into a pocket, brought forth a folded bit of paper. "You got a fellow around here by the name of Starbuck?"

A deep sigh of frustration and hopelessness slipped from Shawn's lips. It had all gone for nothing.

"Starbuck?" Jenner repeated, frowning.

"Yeah. Big man, wearing one of them Mexican hats and a black vest."

"What about him?"

The other outlaws had come to strict attention and were moving in closer to Jenner and the driver. Two of the women were now in the open, and from somewhere back in the hills an eagle cried, breaking the hush that followed the outlaw chief's taut question.

"Stopped me on the road late this morning, give me this here note. Wanted me to have it telegraphed when I got to Jonesboro."

"You read the note?"

"Well, didn't give it no thinking until I got to Jonesboro, then I got to wondering, so I opened it up. Was supposed to go to Bill Granett in Santa Fe. He's the U.S. marshal."

Someone in the group swore loudly. Jenner, a tall, powerful figure in the fading light, stood perfectly still.

"Note's telling him to bring a posse fast

as he could," Booker continued. "Aiming to meet on the road north of here. Was signed by this Starbuck."

"A goddam lawman!" Reo Pierce rose above the hubbub. "A goddam stinking lawman! Knowed all the time there was something haywire about that jasper!"

Jenner reached out a hand to the driver. "That the message?" he asked in a flat voice.

"Sure is. Soon's I read it, I stuck it back in my pocket, borrowed me a horse, and come fast as I could. Figured you'd better know about this."

Starbuck watched as Jenner read the note. He went over it slowly, features pulled into a frown as if trying to understand it.

"This Starbuck been around here long?" the driver asked. "Don't recollect seeing him before."

"Sid took him in a couple a days ago," Pierce said sarcastically. "We all figured him for a double-crosser."

Shawn drew back deeper into the brush. Everything was down the river now; there'd be no posse coming to help round up Jenner and his gang; he was himself a marked man insofar as the outlaws went, destined for a bullet the moment any of them saw him. And outside the valley a like situation existed; he was a dead man there, also.

A wry smile twisted his lips. He was alone — caught in the middle, unable to turn in any direction for help; if anything was to be done about the outlaws, he would have to do it by himself.

"Where the hell is he?"

The fury gripping Sid Jenner had finally surfaced. Crushing the note in his hands, he jammed it into a pocket and moved farther into the yard.

"Ain't come back yet," Reo Pierce replied, a note of satisfaction in his voice.

Gorman bobbed his head. "Told you all the time he was a four-flusher. Like as not he's long gone, and I'm betting he's got that money with him."

"He ain't gone," Jenner said. "Keep remembering he ain't got no friends outside here, either. Chance for going somewheres ain't worth a plugged copper."

"Hell, him being a lawman, they'll let —"

"They don't know that. I figure he's playing this hand alone."

"Folks up in Junction City ain't in on it," Monte said. "Can tell you that for sure. They'd sooner shoot him than draw another breath."

"And if they wasn't, he'd be trying to get word to that deputy or somebody else around there," Kinkaid added.

"That's the way I see it," Jenner said. "My guess is that the only one knowing who he is, is that marshal in Santa Fe."

"Which ain't going to help him much," Rufe said, "him not getting that there telegram sent."

Jenner nodded. "Right. We've got him boxed in tight. Granett just won't ever get the word to bring in his posse."

"Maybe," Kinkaid said laconically. "Reckon we're going to first have to find Starbuck before we can say for sure we got him."

"No sweat there," Rufe said. "We just set tight, let him ride in."

"If he don't already know —" Kinkaid added.

"How the hell'd he know we're onto him? Where could he find out? You ain't seen him again since this morning?"

"Nope," the driver said. "Not since he give me that note and five dollars to do the sending with — that was this morning, late."

Jenner turned to Pierce. "Was you that seen him last. He tell you when he'd be coming in?"

"Only said for you to not keep waiting for him in town if he didn't show up by dark. Said he'd head straight for here." The outlaw paused, studied Jenner narrowly. "Told me you and him had some kind of deal cooking. . . . There something private going on between you and him?"

"What the hell you talking about?" the outlaw chief snapped. "Only deal I've got with him is to dig up that money and bring it in so's we could split it — same as we always do."

"Way he was acting there was more'n that."

Sid Jenner drew up slowly to his full height. "Reo, you calling me a liar?"

A hush had again fallen upon the clearing. Pierce, thumbs hooked in his gun belt, face tipped down, shrugged. "Well, maybe not exactly. Just wondering about it."

"You satisfied?"

"Yeh, reckon I am."

The quiet ran on for another taut minute, broken finally by Kinkaid's lazy drawl. "What're we figuring to do? Ain't no sense standing here gabbling like a bunch of turkeys. We going to start beating the bushes for him or we just setting and waiting?"

"We set and wait," Jenner replied, the tautness now gone from his tone. "He'll be showing up — ain't got no reason not to. Far as he knows, Sam sent that message to the marshal."

"Then where the hell is he?" Gorman shouted angrily. "Doing it all wrong, I figure. We ought to —"

"Like as not he's in town — at Dooley's. Got himself sweet on Clarissa, and he's probably with her right now, along with wetting his whistle after being out there in the hills all day making out he was hunting for that money."

"Yeh, what about that there money?" It was Saul Tinker's voice. "We just going to forget about it?"

"Money? Hell, I bet there never was none," Monte said in disgust. "Was all part of his scheming."

Jenner shook his head. "No, there was the money, all right; know that for a fact. Thing is the bank and the rest of them folks in Junction City wasn't in on his plan to grab it."

"Then you figure it's buried around here somewhere?"

"Stake my share on it — and that's why we're setting tight, let on like we don't know nothing about that message he give

Sam. Want him to think everything's just the same, and then when he shows up after doing his dallying around with Clarissa, we'll nail him."

"And make him talk — tell where the money's hid."

"Right as rain!"

Gorman wagged his head. "Thought you said he was the kind that nobody'd make talk. We was wanting to do that before."

"Sure, but we didn't have no ace in the hole like we've got now."

"Ace? What ace?"

"Clarissa. He ain't going to want to see her get hurt. Some jaspers've got a soft spot when it comes to their women, and I figure he's one. If he thinks we're going to peel a little hide off her, he'll talk right up."

"Then you don't want us out hunting him?" Kinkaid asked.

"Nope, we wait. He'll show up. Like I said, there ain't no reason why he won't."

20

Starbuck withdrew quietly, returned to where he had left the bay. There should be something he could do, he felt, particularly since the outlaws had decided to just lie low, await his arrival at the camp. They would stick with that idea until daylight, probably, and then when there was no sign of him, Sid Jenner would come up with something else.

Disappointed but already casting about in his mind for an alternate plan that would enable him to successfully complete the task he'd undertaken, Shawn mounted his horse. Cutting back down the trail and taking care to pass Maria's as quietly as possible, he continued on until he reached the road. There he halted, uncertain where best to hide out until he could devise a new plan. The thought of giving up had not occurred to him, but he was honest enough with himself to admit that such was inevitable unless he could produce a scheme whereby singlehandedly he could capture Sid Jenner and his men.

He could of course ride to Junction City

and, if lucky, manage to send a telegram to Granett himself; the same applied to Jonesboro, where doing so would be easier since he was not so well known, but it would serve no good purpose. He could expect that by the time the federal lawman arrived with armed men, Sid Jenner and his guns, failing to find him by sundown of that next day and fearing that he had somehow managed to escape from the valley and go for help, would pull out and disappear.

Shaking his head at the thought, he reached down, removed the bits of twigs he had used to wedge the rowels of his spurs into silence, and rode on, crossing the valley to its opposite slope. It was too dark to risk climbing the rough grade to any extent — a horse with a broken leg would certainly mean an end to all he yet hoped to do. Reaching a small coulee, he stopped. Face expressionless as he wrestled with his problem, he squatted on his heels, back to a large boulder, and stared off across the hills, brightening now as the moon gained stature.

It was hard to accept the fact that all he had accomplished could go for nothing. He had been able to work himself into the confidence of Sid Jenner and his gang, become a member, learn the location of their mining camp hideout — all things no one else had ever been able to do. Now, when he had reached the point where such information would enable him to smash the outlaws once and for all time, he was faced with failure. If only he could somehow —

Starbuck came upright slowly, a sense of excitement gripping him. The mine shaft — that was it! Why hadn't it occurred to him before?

But it would take some kind of explosive — dynamite or blasting powder, fuse, and he would still need help at the showdown. To think he could handle Sid Jenner and a half a dozen desperate gunmen who knew that capture meant long terms in the territorial prison, if not the gallows, for their crimes, would be overestimating his abilities.

Where could he get the help and the supplies he must have? He considered his three choices: Junction City, Hackberry, and Jonesboro. The first was his only hope. True, people there believed him to be an outlaw, but that could be cleared up by suggesting they telegraph Bill Granett in Santa Fe. However, considering the mood the people of the town were in, his chances for doing so in person were nil; he would have to leave a note for Beasley or Duckworth.

Beasley. . . . He would be the one since it would be at his store that the explosives and the fuse would be available. He could accomplish both at the sane time — if there was time.

There had to be, he decided grimly. It was his only hope. At once Starbuck went back onto the bay, swung him about and struck for the road. Reaching it, he jammed his spurs into the gelding's flanks, broke him into a fast lope. The round trip, breaking into Beasley's store to get the explosive, and leaving the note would all have to be done before daylight; he had strong doubts the bay could hold up his end of it.

It was near midnight when Shawn reached the edge of the settlement, and pulling his worn horse down to a walk, he skirted the cluster of buildings, all dark except two of the saloons, and rode in behind Beasley's.

He would never make it back on the bay. He realized that when he was still miles from the town, and the only solution to the problem he could think of was to somehow get his own sorrel and make the return trip, which would necessarily have to be covered with speed, on him. The big red gelding was probably at the livery barn where he had stabled him that first day, but he would face the situation when the time came.

Tying the bay to a fence in the deep shadow behind Beasley's, Shawn hurriedly crossed the littered yard and stepped up onto the store's back landing. The two windows and the door were, of course, locked, and moving on, taking care to keep out of the bright moonlight, he circled the building, testing all other such points for a means to enter. They, too, were tightly secured; he would have to force his way in, and that was best done at the rear of the structure.

He chose the window farthest from the adjacent building and, protecting his fist with his bandana, broke the glass a few inches away from the button lock wedging the frames together. The metal slide, rusted from disuse, gave grudgingly, and lifting the lower sash, Shawn slipped inside.

He found himself in a small room, and discovered quickly that cans of blasting powder and coils of fuse were part of what was being stored there. Relieved at his good fortune and thankful he would encounter no delay, he crossed to the door, opened it, and found himself behind the long counter that extended across the back of the wide, well-stocked room.

A sheaf of papers used for wrapping purposes lay immediately to his right. Digging out the stub of pencil carried in a pocket, he wrote a terse note to Beasley on one of the sheets, instructing the merchant to verify first that he was acting under the law and was not a criminal as they supposed. Satisfied, he was to then mount a posse and, following the map drawn on the paper, come as soon as possible.

Placing the message in a prominent place on the counter where it could not be missed, Starbuck returned to the anteroom and helped himself to a coil of fuse and two cans of powder, along with a burlap sack in which to carry the items.

Departing by the same route he had entered, he then hurried back to the bay and swung onto the saddle. The livery stable lay at the opposite end of the street, and again avoiding the saloons, he circled and came in to the squat, square building from the rear. The wide door was open as was usual, and leaving the bay in a pool of darkness, Starbuck hastily entered and began a search of the stalls along the dimly lit runway.

A sigh of relief went through him when he found the sorrel in the third compartment. His gear had been slung across the intervening plank wall, and working fast, he begin to saddle and bridle the gelding.

"What the hell you think you're doing?"

At the harsh question coming from the runway behind him, Starbuck wheeled. It was the hostler.

"Getting my horse," Shawn replied coolly.

"Your horse!" the man echoed. He was holding an old double-barreled shotgun in his hands, the muzzle of which was centered on Starbuck's midsection.

"Sorrel belongs to a fellow that was the sheriff here. Took off —"

The stableman paused, moved a step nearer for closer look. His features were puzzled as he lowered his weapon, leaned forward.

"By Judas, you're him! You're the sheri—"

Shawn's fist connected with the man's jaw. He staggered back, the shotgun falling to the straw-covered floor as he collapsed and went full length on his back.

Starbuck wasted no moments examining the hostler. He was not badly hurt, only unconscious, and would recover shortly. Kicking the old scattergun into the dung at the edge of the runway, he finished with the sorrel and led him to where the weary bay was tied.

Working fast, he transferred the gunny sack to the sorrel's saddle, and then turning the bay loose to fend for himself, he spurred the gelding about and headed south.

The outlaw camp was hours away, and he could only succeed with what he had in mind if he reached there before daylight. But the sorrel was big and strong, and he was fresh. If any horse could do it, he would.

21

Light was showing in the east when Starbuck rode quietly into the first of the old, abandoned mining camps. One hour more and he would have been too late, but thanks to the sorrel, which had scarcely broken stride during the long run, he would be able to proceed with his plan.

Hiding the horse behind one of the shacks on the upper level, Shawn slung the sack of powder and fuse over his shoulder and hurriedly circled the mountain in which Jenner had established his hideout. There were no indications of anyone being up and about as yet; such would not hold true for many more minutes, however; thus, there was no time to be lost.

Reaching the back of the hill, Starbuck moved in quickly to the brush-masked exit of the mine, and working quietly so as to send no echoing sounds carrying along the shaft that would alarm the outlaws at its opposite end, he set the charges of powder. One he placed in the mouth of the opening, the second in the rocks directly above, using a generous amount of the explosive around the well-packed cans so there would be no possibility of failure.

Affixing the fuse, again taking care to avoid any problems, he unrolled the coil, stringing it behind him for its full length as he doubled back toward the entrance to the mine shaft. The fuse played out when he was little more than one-third of the distance. He had hoped to be nearer to the clearing when he applied a match, but it was not to be, and he wasted no time bemoaning the fact.

Making a quick, final inspection of his work and finding all in order, Shawn returned to the end of the fuse and struck fire to the tip. It was fresh merchandise, and the string leaped into life instantly, sparkling fiercely as it rapidly ate its way toward the cans of blasting powder.

He was up and moving at once, hurrying over the rocks as he raced against the fuse to reach a position in the yard where he would have command of the shaft's entrance. The explosion let go just as he gained the edge of the clearing.

The mountain seemed to fly apart on its back slope, and a rush of wind swept across the yard, carrying with it a swirling wall of dust, dry leaves, branches, and other litter. Inside the improvised stable frightened horses began to crash about, but Starbuck gave them no thought. Pistol in hand, he crouched behind one of the weathered, sagging shacks, awaited the reaction that was certain to come from the mine shaft.

His wait was of short duration. As a cloud of dust and smoke belched from the opening, a figure, coughing and gagging, emerged. It was Reo Pierce. Starbuck laid a shot at the outlaw. The bullet sprayed dirt over his feet, caused him to jerk away.

"Get back inside!" Starbuck yelled as the man instinctively clawed at the gun on his hip. "Stay there!"

Pierce retreated slowly for the opening. Others were appearing — two of the women, Sid Jenner himself, Monte, all barely visible in the yellow haze. The rest of the band would be directly behind them.

Starbuck snapped another shot at Pierce's feet. "All of you — stay inside!" he shouted, reloading. "Got a posse coming. We're waiting for them. Anybody tries to break out will run straight into a bullet."

The drifting mixture of smoke and dust appeared to be thinning. It would soon clear inside the shaft, and the outlaws would have no breathing problems while being confined within it. Such could be for several hours, Shawn realized.

Beasley likely would not find the note left for him until he opened his store for business that morning, some time after sunrise. Another hour or two would be lost while he verified matters with Bill Granett in Santa Fe; still more time would be consumed while he organized a posse. He'd be lucky if aid arrived by midafternoon — and keeping the outlaws backed up in the mine shaft for such a long period would prove no easy task.

"Starbuck!"

It was Sid Jenner. Shawn let the call ride until the outlaw chief shouted for him again and then replied.

"Yeh?"

"Don't know what the hell you think you're up to, but it sure ain't going to work," Jenner said in a confident tone.

"Maybe it will."

"Me, I know better. Posse you're looking for ain't going to make it."

"Don't take any bets on that."

"It's a fact. Best you play it smart, let us out of here."

"Not about to. Took a lot of hard work getting you and your outfit to where the law can step in, take over. Be a waste to turn you loose now."

"I'm willing to deal with you. You back off, and I'll let you ride out, even if you are a lawman. What you don't know is that the posse you sent for never got the word, so it won't be showing up."

"Know that," Shawn said calmly. "Not expecting them. Happens there's another bunch on the way."

Jenner fell silent, evidently surprised that Starbuck was aware that his telegram to Bill Granett had not been sent.

The haze had all but disappeared, and he could now see shadowy movements within the dark entrance to the mine. By that time the outlaws had undoubtedly made their way to the exit on the far side of the mountain in the hope of finding that escape route still open. They would have met only disappointment, he was certain; the amount of blasting powder he had used was sure to have dislodged a large segment of the slope and blocked the hole.

Abruptly, gunshots broke out from the entrance to the shaft. Bullets slammed into the shed behind which Starbuck crouched. The outlaws were trying to break out make a dash to freedom. Leveling his weapon, Shawn drove three quick shots at the mine entrance. Eyes on the opening, he again reloaded.

No one ventured into view. They had been testing him, seeing how good their chances would be if they poured a covering barrage of bullets into the old shack.

"Wasting lead," he drawled. "Just sit back and take it easy."

There was no answer from the mine shaft. Starbuck glanced over his shoulder. The sun was well up and beginning its climb into the clean sky. Beasley by that time should have his confirmation from the U.S. marshal, might possibly have his posse in the saddle and on the road.

Movement at the shaft's entrance drew his attention. Raising his pistol, he triggered a bullet into the rocky surface directly above the opening. Whoever it was jerked back. Again punching out the spent cartridge, Starbuck inserted a fresh shell in the cylinder of his weapon. It was wise to keep the forty-five fully loaded at all times in the remote event that they should attempt to rush him.

Keeping his eyes on the mine entrance, he waited for further signs of movement, but none came, and after a time, he settled down once more to ride out the dragging minutes.

He had earlier considered allowing the outlaws to step out one by one, throwing their weapons off into the brush as they emerged, and thereby allow them the greater comfort of being in the open. He had decided against it. It was much easier to keep them bottled up inside the mine even though they still had their guns. The danger of his somehow being overcome by them was much less while they were confined to a place where there was but one exit.

The mine would clear of dust and smoke, if it had not already done so, and being compelled to remain inside would do them no harm — not that it mattered particularly to him, but it was unfortunate that the women were also trapped.

He could make no exception there, either; if he permitted them to leave, any one of the four, faithful to Sid Jenner and the other men, could easily smuggle out a weapon and at the first opportunity turn it on him. . . . He stirred wearily, glanced again at the sun. It seemed to have come to a standstill in the arching sweep of blue.

A spate of firing again broke out, and for a few moments, the thud of bullets driving into the old shed was like the pounding of rain on a roof. He waited until it was over, made his answer with two shots aimed generally at the shaft's entrance, reloaded. They were testing him once again; his reply would assure them that he was alive and still on guard.

"Starbuck!"

"Right here, Sid."

"You better be doing what I said. Time's running out."

"For you and your bunch, not me," Shawn countered. "Country's been waiting for this day. Glad it's finally here."

"It ain't over yet," Jenner said. "I've been in tights like this before, always come out. Plenty of times."

"Expect this is some different. You're boxed in and trying to get out of there can only get you killed."

"Reckon not. Always got me an ace in the hole, and it won't be long till I'll be playing it. Giving you your last chance."

"Forget it, Sid. It's all over for you —"

"Guess again, you goddam, lousy badge toter!"

Alarm whipped through Starbuck. It was Rufe Gorman's voice! Understanding flooded into his mind. Not all of the outlaws had been inside the shaft. He had made a bad mistake, one that could be his last. He began to turn slowly.

"Stay put." It was the drawling Tex Kinkaid. "Sure would pleasure me plenty to put a bullet in your head right where you're setting for crossing us like you done, but I reckon Sid wouldn't like that — leastwise not till he's through with you. . . . Drop that gun."

22

Starbuck allowed his pistol to fall to the ground, remained motionless. Boot heels thudded, and a moment later Kinkaid reached down, claimed the weapon.

"Now get up," he ordered.

Shawn rose slowly, mind working feverishly as he sought a means out of the pocket he was suddenly in. From nearby, Gorman's hoarse voice broke the quiet.

"It's all right, Sid — we got him! Brung the gal, too."

Starbuck frowned, half turned. Clarissa, Rufe's arm about her waist, a hairy hand clamped over her mouth to prevent any outcry while he and Kinkaid closed in, was staring at him helplessly. As he yelled, the outlaw released the girl, shoved her roughly at him.

Shawn caught her as she stumbled, gripped her tight to prevent her from falling. He saw no fear in her eyes, only anger.

"You're plenty tough with women," he snapped.

Rufe grinned, pointed toward the mine. "Get over there, both of you."

Starbuck, Clarissa a half a step behind him, moved out into the open. Jenner, all of the remaining outlaws, and the women had come from the shaft, were clustered before its entrance. Some were coughing, hawking to clear their throats; others were wiping at the sweat-soaked dust caked on their faces and necks. Reo Pierce, anger boiling over suddenly, took a long stride toward Shawn.

"Goddam you — you —"

Jenner, only his small, hard eyes revealing the rage that filled him, caught the outlaw by the arm, pulled him back.

"Forget it," he snapped, and bucked his head at the women gathered in a small group. "Pack up. We're getting out of here."

"What for?" Pierce demanded instantly. "We got him. Ain't no use running now."

"I figure there is," Jenner replied coldly. "I don't know if he was stringing us about another posse coming or not. Hardly think so — and anyway, I ain't for taking any chance on it. He wouldn't've just laid out there behind that shed if he wasn't looking for help to come."

"Could've been bluffing and figuring on

pulling out when he got the chance," Jubal said.

Jenner, his small, dark eyes fixed steadily upon Starbuck, shrugged. "Maybe and maybe not. Like I said, we don't take the chance. Aim to move on, set up a watch from down the canyon a ways. Posse shows, we'll keep going; if it don't, then we'll come back."

The women were already turning back into the mine to do the outlaw chief's bidding; the men, watching Shawn and Clarissa with narrow expectancy, stood about in a loose circle, enclosing them.

Starbuck shifted his attention to the girl. "Didn't aim for you to get dragged into this."

Her shoulders stirred slightly. "Was my fault for letting them get hold of me. . . . What do they want me for?"

"Figure to use you to make me tell where I cached that bank money."

Clarissa gazed thoughtfully at Jenner. "I would expect that from him, all right," she murmured. "Nothing matters to Sid except getting what he wants."

Shawn considered that in silence while the belief that there existed more than the usual saloon girl-outlaw relationship between the two again occurred to him.

"You should've listened to me, Sheriff," Jenner said, turning to face Starbuck. "Been smart to've taken me up on my offer. I had you hands down all the way."

Shawn realized that now. Kinkaid and Gorman had probably spent the night, or most of it, in Hackberry watching for him. When he did not show, they had headed back to the camp, forcing Clarissa to go with them, thinking that he had perhaps returned during their absence. Jenner had warned them that something was wrong by opening up with gunfire — gunfire he had mistaken as attempts to escape and tests of his vigilance.

Amy, followed by Myrtha, Abby, and Fay, appeared in the mouth of the mine shaft, and filed into the open. They were carrying rolled-up blankets, saddlebags, socks, and hastily gathered bits of clothing and personal belongings. Jenner flicked them with a glance.

"Get that stuff loaded on the horses," he said to Jubal. And then motioning to Saul Tinker, added, "Give him a hand. We'll be pulling out of here in a bit."

The two outlaws wheeled irritably, moved toward the stable with the women trailing behind them. Jubal paused, looked back.

"What about the spare horses?"

"Turn them loose, can round them up later," Jenner said, and faced Starbuck. "Your last chance, so tell me where you hid that cash. You take it, I'll let the woman go. You don't, and I'll use her to open your mouth."

Starbuck glanced off to the east, to the direction in which the road lay. He had missed by hours, thus failed completely. Beasley and a posse, if one was en route, could not be anywhere near yet, and with Clarissa — no matter if he was only barely acquainted with her — in the hands of the outlaws, he was beaten.

Shrugging, he said, "Let her go."

Jenner smiled. "Sure, just as soon as you do some talking," he said smoothly.

"No deal. She rides out first."

"Who the hell he think he is?" Gorman shouted. "He ain't giving no orders!"

Monte nodded, stepped up beside the outlaw chief. "Wasting time. Let me stake out the gal. I start working on her, I'll have him bleating like a nanny goat."

"Won't need to go that far," Jenner said. "He ain't the kind to let a woman get hurt. . . . One of you get a horse for her."

"You letting her go?" Gorman demanded angrily, his dark features shining with sweat.

"After me and Tex went to all the bother of bringing her up her so's we —"

"She's going," Jenner cut in coldly.

"The hell she is! Maybe you're damn fool enough to take this bastard's word that he'll tell where the money's hid, but I ain't! We're hanging onto her till we've got that cash right in our hands!"

Sid Jenner whirled. "You've been pushing hard for this, Rufe!" he said in a savage tone, and seizing Gorman by the arm, swung him hard into the face of the cliff.

The outlaw struck the solid surface of rock with sickening force. A yell burst from his flaring lips as he rebounded, staggered, went sprawling full length to the ground.

"Now, hold on!" Kinkaid said protestingly. "Way I see it, Rufe's right."

Stepping forward, he moved toward the stunned Gorman, cutting between Starbuck and the other outlaws. Shawn reacted instantly. Lunging, he jerked Kinkaid's pistol from its holster, knocking the girl to one side and out of harm's way as he did. In the same motion he shoved the drawling Texan into Monte and Reo Pierce.

Jenner cursed, whipped out his gun. Starbuck, bent low and spinning, fired fast, drove the outlaw to his knees with a bullet in his chest. Continuing to move, he triggered the weapon again, shooting point blank at Pierce and then Monte. Both men went down.

Kinkaid had found a weapon, probably Gorman's, and was throwing himself across his friend, twisting and firing as he moved. Starbuck felt the sear of a bullet as it ripped through a sleeve, sliced a groove across his forearm. He snapped a shot at the Texan, saw him jolt, fall away.

He had one, possibly two bullets left in the pistol. There were still Jubal, Saul Tinker, and the dazed Rufe Gorman, now struggling to rise, to account for. Pivoting, he saw Tinker running toward him through the coiling layers of smoke, fired. The outlaw rocked to one side as a splash of red appeared on his neck. The bullet had only grazed him. Starbuck, ducking away to offer no target for the man's own weapon, triggered his pistol again, heard only the dull click of the hammer falling on an empty cylinder.

Tinker, his features split in a hard grin, raised his pistol. From the shack where the horses were kept Jubal was shouting: "Shoot him, goddammit — shoot him!"

Tinker continued to hang motionless,

eyes turned toward the edge of the clearing where the trail pressed close to the side of the mountain. He seemed to be frozen, caught up by something he saw there. Gorman, too, on his feet now, was silent.

Starbuck threw a hurried glance over his shoulder, drew a long breath of relief. Beasley, Deputy Troy Egan, a half a dozen more men, all with rifles, were breaking out of the brush.

The posse. . . .

23

Starbuck sleeved away the sweat beading his forehead, watched the members of the posse move in swiftly and take charge. He didn't know how they had managed to get there so quickly, but they had, and that was all that counted. Now none of the Jenner gang would escape.

Crossing to the outlaw leader's side, he picked up his pistol, glanced at the stilled features. He was dead. Shrugging, he turned back to where Clarissa stood. Out in the center of the clearing Egan and his men were herding the three remaining outlaws and the women into a small cluster and tying their hands behind their backs. Myrtha was objecting loudly, emphasizing her opposition to being thus treated with strong language.

"You all right?" Starbuck asked the girl.

Clarissa stirred wearily. "I suppose so."

Beasley came up smiling broadly. "Got 'em all, I see. Which one's Jenner?"

Starbuck pointed to the outlaw. "One next to him's Reo Pierce. Others are

Kinkaid and Monte. Had no choice but to shoot."

"No matter," Beasley said cheerfully. "We got three we can try and hang." He paused, extended a hand to Starbuck. "Got you to thank for this."

"Was my job —"

"Had us fooled there at first. Figured you'd for sure had throwed in with them. Should've known it was what you were planning to do. Reckon you got an apology coming."

"No need. It was how I wanted it — you not trusting me. It was the only way I could get in with Jenner and be certain he believed me. . . . I ought to be thanking you, however. Didn't think there was a chance of you getting here until noon or later."

"Probably wouldn't have if I hadn't found that note you left. Howie, the night holster at the livery stable, come and rousted me out of bed after you knocked him cold and rode off on your horse. On the way I seen that window you busted in the back of my store and went in. Came across your note with the map drawned on it first thing."

"You telegraph Granett?"

"Didn't bother. Came to me right then

what you'd been up to all the time, so I rounded up Egan, and we got a posse mounted and then lit out fast."

"Almost got here too late," the deputy said, stepping up and offering his hand.

Shawn nodded to the lawman, accepted the courtesy. "Was a mite close," he admitted, his attention on Clarissa. She had moved to where Jenner lay, was looking down at him.

"Who's she?" Beasley asked quietly, taking note.

"Name's Clarissa. Saloon girl from Hackberry."

"She part of Jenner's bunch?"

Shawn was silent for a time. Then, "No, friend of mine. They were going to use her to make me tell where I hid the money."

"The bank's money!" Beasley said, as if suddenly remembering. "It safe?"

Starbuck nodded, eyes still on Clarissa, seemingly unable to turn away from the dead outlaw. "I'll show you where it is when we head back. It probably was Grimshaw's bookkeeper tipping Jenner off. Stagecoach driver by the name of Booker's mixed up in it, too. May be others. . . . You all get mounted up. We'll be along in a minute."

Beasley and Egan turned to rejoin the

rest of the posse, now getting horses ready for their prisoners. Starbuck crossed to the girl's side, touched her lightly on the arm.

"Time we were leaving —"

Motionless, she continued to stare at Jenner. "Aren't they going to bury him — and the others?" she asked finally.

"Probably pack the bodies in to Hackberry, give them a proper burial there. It mean something to you?"

Clarissa looked up at him. There was a hint of tears in her eyes. "Sid was my husband," she said simply. "We parted soon after we came here."

Her words brought understanding to Starbuck. He knew now why none of the other outlaws would have anything to do with Clarissa, why Jenner had discouraged his interest in her, and why, despite the fact that it had been the man's own idea to bring her to the camp for the purpose of forcing him to talk, in the end he had refused to let Gorman and the others harm her.

"Because of what he was?"

"Of what he became. He was a good man once, but the war ruined him just as it does most everything. . . . I would have gone back home long ago if he would have let me, but he was afraid I'd talk, bring the law down on him. I wouldn't have, of course."

Starbuck shook his head. "That's all over and done with — finished for good. There's no one to stop you now," he said gently, and taking her by the hand, he led her across the clearing to where the others waited.